FORGERY IN RED

JUDITH CAMPBELL

Forgery in Red

The First Viridienne Greene Mystery

Published in the United States of America
~Fine. Line. Press~
Highland Terrace
Plymouth, Massachusetts, 02360
www.judithcampbell-holymysteries.com

To Chris-Frederick, husband, first reader, editor/nitpicker in chief, I salute you, and I thank you for the endless cups of coffee, your encouragement, understanding, and most of all, your abiding friendship and support. Twenty-five years and counting... how did we get so lucky?

Introduction

"Aedh Wishes for the Cloths of Heaven"

Had I the heavens' embroidered cloths,
Enwrought with golden and silver light,
The blue and the dim and the dark cloths
Of night and light and the half light,
I would spread the cloths under your feet:
But I, being poor, have only my dreams;
I have spread my dreams under your feet;
Tread softly because you tread on my dreams.

William Butler Yeats. It was published in 1899 in his third volume of poetry, *The Wind Among the Reeds.*

Prologue

✻

Feature Story

ART COLLECTORS AROUND THE WORLD ARE OVERJOYED to learn of the discovery of five uncatalogued Nicolo Brandosi paintings. The paintings, fully authenticated, were found in a long-unused family-vacation cottage located in the Adirondacks.

Custodian and curator of the paintings, the artist's brother Giovanni Brandosi, is quoted as saying, "When the fame and the publicity and the fast life got too much for my brother, he'd go out there and get away for a couple of weeks. He'd chop his own wood, eat beans out of cans, and paint until the sun went down. He was obsessed with his art. We had no idea he'd left anything out there. We found the paintings when we were getting ready to sell the place."

The paintings will be cataloged and offered for sale at auction at a future date.

Chapter One

The man wearing jeans and a dark hoodie stood well back in the shadows and waited until it was fully dark before starting down the street toward her house. He'd parked the car two blocks away and moved quickly to where the ragged, untrimmed privet hedge marked the borders of the property. From there, he slipped into an open space in the foliage where a short man like himself could be completely hidden from view. He'd practiced this so many times that every movement was automatic. When he finally made his move, he would have only one chance to get it right.

He stopped, listening for footsteps or the sound of an oncoming car, then ducked his head, pushed through the other side of the overgrown hedge, and paced out the twenty-two steps from the greenery to the back of the tree. Using a pole climber's harness for support, he hiked himself up to the first great branch divide, a place where he could see directly into her studio. He let go of the breath he'd been holding and leaned forward, resting his body against a familiar spot. Slowly and carefully, so as not to lose his balance, he slipped a pair of binoculars and a camera out of his pocket.

There she was, standing motionless in front of her latest work—deep in thought, brush in hand, barely breathing, contemplating her next move. She was so beautiful—and unaware that she had little time left. The die had been cast, and the only moves were forward. The next time he came back, the deed would be over and done with, and he would be free of the burden he'd carried for close to half his life.

Feeling the winter cold more acutely than ever, the man leaned even closer to the branch to get out of the wind and watched as the painting on the easel came to life. The woman did a kind of dance with each one, a ritual pas de deux between artist and canvas. A touch here, a swipe and a dab there, then a quick slash of color joining the two... often followed by an impatient rub with the rag she always held in her left hand. And then came the contemplative pause. It all looked so random and unplanned. But it wasn't. This kind of apparent spontaneity was the result of years of practice... of painting alone in silence, behind closed doors.

He, more than anyone—except maybe that weird-looking friend of hers, Viridienne Greene—knew the skill and passion that went into those staggering paintings. The real question was, how much did she know? That could be a problem. If there was even a hint of trouble coming from Viridienne Greene, he knew where to find her. But he would only act on that if necessary. *No point in shooting your ducks before they're lined up.* At the moment, it was enough to know there could possibly be more than one player in this deadly game.

"Forewarned is forearmed," his grandfather used to say. His grandfather, well-known in his own lifetime, took no prisoners.

He peeled back the sleeve of his jacket and looked at his watch. It was almost time. Snow was forecast for the next couple of days, but that was a good thing. Snow meant fewer people on the streets and looking out their windows. Meanwhile, the cold night air was getting to him. He wiped his nose on his sleeve and started inching back down and out of the tree.

IN ANOTHER PART OF TOWN, A TALL, THIN GREY-HAIRED woman, Viridienne Greene, was frantically working to meet a deadline. The drop-off day for the Mayflower Artists and Artisans Winter Art Show was in less than two days, and she was far from finished. Fiber arts were not something you could rush to complete, no matter how good you were. But try as she might, she couldn't start working toward a deadline any earlier. It was just how she operated. The design that was developing in Viridienne Greene's mind and struggling to take shape under her practiced fingers always remained out of reach until the submission deadline for the next show was breathing down her slender neck. She would finish in time—she knew that. She always did. It would take a coffee-laced all-nighter. Once again, she wished for a fleeting moment that she were as disciplined as her friend Rose. Someone had once described Viridienne and Rose as "chalk and cheese"—as different as two women could be. Maybe that was what made their friendship work.

Rose Doré was a diminutive first-generation Greek-American powerhouse of a painter with a past as dark and turbulent as her magnificent paintings. The two women were close in age, both nearer to forty than thirty. And while they had much in common with one another, they had just as much that was polar opposite. They were both creative, determined women artists who had been betrayed by God and family but who, after time, had managed to transcend the darkness of the past through their art.

Viridienne was tall, rangy, and fair skinned and moved like a great blue heron—slow and deliberate... until she struck. Rose was quick moving, small, and muscular, though she was becoming softer around the edges and rounder in the tummy as she approached middle age. She had the dark hair, dark skin, and piercing dark eyes that had been determined by the gods and goddesses of her heritage, and she wore them well.

Rose worked in oils and occasionally acrylics, producing large-scale semi-abstract and abstract expressionist pieces that staggered the mind and the eye of the viewer. Viridienne was a fiber artist, a collector of bits of yarn, scraps of fabric, and pieces of strings too short to use. These were the castoffs she worked into her weavings and assemblages in a way that demanded that the viewer stop, look more deeply, and engage in the visual dialog that she'd set in motion with her long, strong fingers.

The two women, whose lives had become connected

and eventually intertwined through their art and secrets, first met at the Mayflower Gallery. They literally crashed into each other coming through the front door, delivering work for the annual members' winter show. After hasty and embarrassed apologies, they backed up and took turns holding the door open and helping each other with their precious cargo. After almost a year of working side by side —and stopping for an occasional coffee or a glass of wine in the late afternoon—their cautious acquaintance had worked its way into a deep and abiding friendship.

Now, with the holidays—which they both loathed—safely behind them and intermittent snow forecast for the next several days, the two women were fully engaged in preparing pieces for the upcoming winter exhibit. With two days to go, Rose was doing the final touch-up before she added her signature. Viridienne was just getting started.

Chapter Two

Viridienne Greene was the name that Obedient Charity had chosen at the age of eighteen years when she slipped out the back door and escaped from the Society of Obedient Believers to begin a new life. Obedient Charity was the name Carol Jensen had been given when her parents renounced the world and its pleasures and became lifelong members of the Society of Obedient Believers. Locked away for years in a rigid and strictly ordered community, Carol never forgot the world beyond the walls of the community. She remembered music and brightly colored crayons and birthday cakes and jump-rope songs. She remembered when her parents used to laugh. She remembered her little sister, Obedient Thankful, born after her family had become Obedient Believers, as being her only plaything—a living doll-baby. Make-believe dolls, toys, and other distractions from the outside world were not allowed. From the day that little Thankful was born, Charity cherished and tried to protect her. At the last moment, she almost didn't leave because of her.

On the day after Charity's coming-of-age birthday—when she legally became an independent adult in the state of California—she packed up the few things she'd managed hide inside her mattress and slipped away from the society forever. It wasn't easy. She'd been planning her escape for months... years really. Her new life would begin miles away from the compound. She was terrified at the prospect and, at the same time, breathless with anticipation. She knew little of the outside world, but the young woman formerly known as Obedient Charity was a quick study. If she'd learned anything in her time in the compound, it was survival. She knew all about protective coloration, blending in, keeping her head down, not attracting any kind of attention, and keeping her thoughts and words to herself.

The night she left for good, she feigned illness at dinner and asked if she could go up to bed early. Alone in her room, she used the classic ruse of stuffing things under the blanket to resemble a sleeping form. She went so far as to cut off her waist-length hair and leave it tangled on the pillow—the way her own hair looked at night when she released it from its tightly braided constraints.

Then, shorn like frightened lamb, she waited on the upper landing until she was assured the other members of the extended family were gathered for ritual evening prayers. When all was quiet, like a phantom in the mist, she slipped out of the door and ran off into the night.

When she reached the end of the unmarked road that led to the compound, she stopped, waiting. A woman named Grace had slipped her a note months earlier when she'd been on the outside, helping with a delivery: "If you need help, call me." The note included a phone number. Obedient Charity decided to trust the woman—and her own instincts—and in secret had begun the conversations that led her to where she now stood in the cool night air, watching for headlights. She reached up, rubbed the prickly stubble on the back of her head, and smiled. For the first time in her life, even her head felt free.

NOT UNTIL THE FOLLOWING MORNING, WHEN OBEDIENT Charity's mother went upstairs to the sleeping rooms to check on her daughter's whereabouts, was the absence discovered. The motionless human-shaped lump under the quilt and the detached tangle of hair that fell to the floor when she touched the sheet told the story. The stoic woman bit her lip and clenched her fists in wordless grief. Rules were rules. Without a sound, she reached down and gathered up a few strands of her daughter's hair, wound them around her finger into a tight spiral, and stuffed the little coil deep into her apron pocket. Then, dry-eyed and forever silent in her disobedience, she went back downstairs and informed the others.

Later that day, by the time everyone had been notified of the change in their number, Obedient Charity's name had already been removed from the community census and all existing records. Her remaining few items of clothing were burned and buried. If her parents were in shock or grieving, they never showed it. Obedient Thankful only asked once about her missing sister and was severely disciplined for doing so. She never spoke her name again. Even though she memorized the message she'd found in her jacket pocket the day after Charity left, she kept the precious scrap of paper folded and taped to the underside of the bottom drawer of her dresser. It was the only tangible proof that her beautiful, spirited, impish sister had ever lived.

After the departure of Obedient Charity, life in the enclave of the Society of Obedient Believers continued without so much as a ripple. The dark, silent waters closed over the empty place, and her name was never mentioned again. The elders renewed their warnings of the dangers of the world beyond the walls and increased the penalties and punishments for any infraction of the rules.

Obedient Thankful lived in silent sadness and constant fear. For her to tell anyone she missed her sister would be unthinkable. And to make matters worse, she was approaching her own transition into womanhood. She could feel the eyes—and on more than one occasion, the hands—of some of the elders. More silence. More shame. But underneath it all, her determination grew. One day, she too would break free.

Chapter Three

Once out and away from the compound, the woman who would become Viridienne Greene knew she would never once think of going back —nor would anyone try to find her. Everyone understood that if a member left the society, all knowledge about that person would be expunged. Leaving was worse than death, because at least families on the outside were allowed to mourn their dead. Inside the compound, life would go on as though nothing had happened.

At age eighteen years and one day, Obedient Charity took a deep breath and ran like hell down the dirt road to start her new life. In the beginning, the world outside the compound was terrifying. Obedient Charity, aka Viridienne Greene, really was a stranger in a strange land. But as she would remind herself, she was safe, she had food to eat, and she had a place to live. With the help of the skilled, understanding staff and volunteers at the shelter where she was first taken, she found a low-stress job and was soon able to pay a modest rent. That was the easy part. After eighteen years of enforced obedience to a false god, discovering the woman she really was would likely take the rest of her life. Viridienne knew in her heart that if she had the inner strength to make it this far, that same fortitude and resilience would be her salvation in the future. No more God talk, no more Jesus platitudes, no more Elder James with his wandering hands, watching and waiting to catch her alone. No more whippings, no more days on stale bread and water, no more dark, humiliating nights that were never mentioned in the light of day. She was free. Though she was anxious and had a lot to learn, Viridienne was not afraid.

Her new life was a daily learning adventure. Over the weeks and months, she learned how to use computers and negotiate the Internet. She learned how to manage her money and talk, look, and dress like the women around her. Her limited spare time she spent at the local library, learning all she could about schools and colleges as well as housing costs and availability on the opposite coast.

When the day came that she felt ready to move on, she thanked everyone for all they had done for her and bought herself a one-way bus ticket to Boston, independence, and freedom. She'd chosen Boston because it appeared to be a city of a manageable size that offered all of the opportunities necessary to her future. That, and it was an entire continent away from her past life in rural Northern California. She settled there, found a steady job, and within a year, managed to get herself accepted to the Massachusetts College of Art with a major in fiber art and design.

When she was little, before she was locked away in the

compound, her favorite playthings had been scraps of yarn and bits of ribbon and the fabric cuttings she swept up and salvaged from her mother's sewing room. In art school, she was able to put a name to that passion and begin her life-long love affair with fabric and fiber. Truly, the artist she was born to be was emerging from her cocoon.

As a child, she'd learned just how dark and unforgiving a human being could be, and with that in mind, she was guarded in her movements and slow to trust. Cautiously, the woman with no past created her own brave new world and peopled it with those cherished few who made the effort to get to know her. One of those was Rose Doré, another artist with a dark past.

Chapter Four

A few years after graduating from art school, Viridienne decided she was ready to leave the comfort and familiarity of Boston and strike out on her own. After some research, she decided to try her luck in the historic coastal town of Plymouth, Massachusetts. Its selling points were that it was commutable to Boston, she could walk to almost everything she would need, and the summer influx of tourists would provide a constant and changing market for her work.

Before long, she'd located an attic apartment in a multiple dwelling near the center of town. It offered three big rooms, great light, and boasted of a "winter water view." Translation: when the leaves fell from the trees, if she stood on tiptoe, she could see about four inches of Plymouth harbor from her bedroom window. And she was allowed to have a cat. She took the place sight unseen and planned on getting herself a cat as soon as she was settled. Meanwhile, she decided to practice by caring for a plant left behind by the previous tenants. Viridienne was taking life one step at a time.

If anyone asked, she would have said she was almost content and often happy with her lot in life. The qualifying *almost* and *often* were in reference to the memories and haunting images of her early life and her fragile younger sister. Until the night she escaped, Viridienne had done her best to protect Thankful from the ever-present dangers that surrounded her and all women in the community. Her sister had still been a little girl when Viridienne left the compound. With years and miles between the two of them, Viridienne could only hope she had managed to survive and find some measure of happiness.

The memories of her escape remained vivid. When she least expected, they came rushing back as a reminder that she had unfinished business in Northern California. On nights when she couldn't sleep, she would replay the details of her escape. She recalled creeping into the back hallway of the big house, step by quivering step, and pushing the scrap of paper deep into the pocket of Thankful's jacket, which was hanging beside the others on a row of identical pegs beside the rear outside door. The message said, "Dearest little sister, if you ever want to find me, I'll be somewhere on the other side of the country. I will have a color for a name. I don't know which one yet. I'll try to find a way to let you know. Burn this note. They will punish you if they find it. I will always love you."

She shook her head and fought back the tears. *One day maybe.* She sighed and pulled herself back into the present.

"Soon," she whispered to the remembered image of her sister. "I won't forget you—I promise."

Chapter Five

After she got settled into her apartment, it didn't take Viridienne long to find herself a cat and begin working her way into the Southeastern Massachusetts art scene. Within two years, she, Old Deuteronomy—the shelter cat she'd adopted—and the spider plant were permanent residents of Plymouth. Her income was growing steadily enough for her to consider becoming a homeowner. She was ready to be done with rentals, housing insecurity, and landlord-imposed restrictions. So instead of even thinking about going to church on a Sunday or any other day of the week, she religiously read the real estate advertisements. There was not much out there that fit her limited budget, but once again, Viridienne had done her homework. From time to time, sad little fixer-uppers came on the market, and when that happened, a person had to be quick. Four rooms—or even five—would be adequate for her, the cat, and the plant.

Viridienne had no intention of sharing that sacred

space with anyone or anything else. The thought of having a significant other had crossed her mind on more than one occasion, but the inconvenience, messiness, and entanglements that defined most personal relationships were more than she could bear. The cat and the plant were all she could handle.

It took half a year of looking, but eventually, Viridienne found the house of her dreams—and her pocketbook. The abandoned, neglected, uninsulated 1930s pondside summer cottage was advertised as a fixer-upper bordering the Miles Standish State Forest, not ten miles from where she was presently living. Two weeks later, she owned it. From day one, the house was both a rescue mission and a labor of love. She got it for back taxes because it was ugly, overgrown with bittersweet and bindweed, and infested with an active colony of mice in the cupboards and closets. No other sane person could possibly have wanted it. *Destiny*, she thought. *This house and I both need work.* Through the metaphoric process of rescue and reconstruction, Viridienne would add another skill to her resume: carpentry.

She named the place the Lily Pad, and the very first thing she did before moving in was to make a painted sign to hang over the front door. The little house was everything she needed: four small rooms topped off with a dusty, creaky, leaky crawl space of an attic with the rusty, tattered remains of a screened-in porch along one entire side, overlooking Skye Pond. It needed a lot of TLC and even more elbow grease. *Game on!*

Shortly after moving in, she decided to knock out the wall between the two north-facing bedrooms to make a large, bright working studio. *Who needs a whole room just to sleep in?* she asked herself, sledgehammer in hand.

"Not me!" she said aloud then gave a war whoop and took the first unpracticed, mighty swing at the dividing wall between the two rooms. The cat, unprepared for the thunderous assault on his new digs, yowled and bolted for cover.

The wall was soon history, the rubble was cleared away, and the plant was washed and rehung. The cat eventually came out of hiding to inspect and purr his approval. *Food and a shower, in reverse order*, thought Viridienne. *In my own home!*

Her sleeping area would be an oversized pullout sofa in a corner of the living room. This she shared with her cat and no one else. The sofa bed, when opened, could accommodate two consenting adults, but even after all these years, Viridienne was still not ready to open herself to any kind of intimacy. She'd risked going out on a couple of dates since moving to Plymouth, but the brief encounters were spectacularly unsuccessful. With that in mind, she put the efforts into an imaginary folder marked "Further Study" and moved it to the back of the drawer.

What she had was more than enough. She owned a forever nest—a home base where she could do her work and entertain one or two selected friends when she so chose. When she shut and locked the door behind her, even the terrible memories couldn't get in.

It was from here that she slowly began to make a place for herself in the larger South Shore, Cape, and Islands arts community. She started by joining a local group calling itself the Mayflower Artists and Artisans—the MAA. The group had a gallery where she could display her work, do a little teaching to earn some money, and socialize with other area artists. At the end of the day, she could go home and lose herself in her work, literally tying up the threads and weaving in the loose ends of her creations. Finally, Viridienne had a home, and although she was a declared atheist, she considered the Lily Pad holy—a place of safety and sanctuary.

But at that moment, on a cold day in early January, she needed to be done with her time-wasting reflections and mindless games of computer solitaire. She needed to get moving on her latest creation for the winter show. This time, she really had procrastinated for too long. For the first time in her professional career, she stood in danger of missing the deadline completely. The cat and the spider plant remained silent, but she knew what they were thinking.

Chapter Six

❧❦❧

U pstairs in an enormous old Victorian house in one of the older, more established neighborhoods of Plymouth, Viridienne Greene's one true friend, Rose Doré, was poking aimlessly around her studio. She would pick up a brush or a tube of paint only to put it down somewhere else. She was distracted, thinking—obsessing really—about one of the three paintings she'd chosen for the MAA winter show. She was giving it a mental once-over and questioning her decision to submit it. *Is it really finished? Is there something else I need to do?*

She was a well-known perfectionist. On more than one occasion, after a show had been judged and hung, she'd slipped back into the gallery at night and made a couple of last-minute changes. Most likely, only she would know or care… unless of course someone accidentally touched the surface and smeared the still-wet paint. Whatever the case, she was obsessive enough that she'd done it before and, if necessary, would do it again.

No, I'll do it right now. She'd call Jackson Smith and ask him to pick the painting up and bring it back. Rose wiped her hands, took off the splotched butcher apron she wore in the studio, and reached for her phone. The gallery would be closed, of course, but Jackson had a key. She'd make the changes and have him pick it up early the next day. The piece would be back in place long before the volunteers and the judges arrived, and no one at all would be the wiser for it.

There! She congratulated herself, symbolically wiping her hands of the issue. Problem solved. She'd pay Jackson for his time. She always did. It worked for all concerned. He was able to earn a little pocket money here and there by doing odd jobs for several people at the gallery, and in turn, they had someone they could trust with those pesky little jobs that everyone hated. He got them done—and done well.

Chapter Seven

☙

The first indication that all was not going according to plan was on Thursday morning, when the hanging committee couldn't find one of the three paintings submitted by Rose Doré. Ordinarily, this would not have been a problem. Things got misplaced and then they got unmisplaced... it was the way of the world and certainly not uncommon in the well-intentioned, often disorganized all-volunteer MAA.

This was not true with Rose and her much-admired and often-envied paintings. Nothing was ever late, forgotten in haste, or misplaced. They all knew she might come back and touch one up, but she was never late in having it delivered. She was an extraordinary artist and as demanding of herself as she was of others. That someone of her ability had chosen to live in and work in staid, historic, out-of-the-artistic-mainstream Plymouth rather than rise and shine in trendy New York or Seattle was a mystery, one of those things people wondered about behind closed doors but never asked her directly.

Rose didn't encourage or invite direct questions. She was always pleasant and friendly, especially with children, but even with them, she held herself apart. She donated hours upon hours to the art association and attended most of the events, but there was an invisible fence around her that said, "You can come this far but no closer." It was as though her life, as much as anyone knew about it, had begun when she'd moved to Plymouth seven years earlier. She didn't speak of her life before the move to anyone other than Viridienne Greene. And Viridienne would have had her toenails pulled out before she'd betray a confidence. She was like that—fiercely loyal to people she cared about… and every bit as private about her own past. They made a good pair.

Viridienne had as many secret passages and closed doors in her life as Rose Doré did. Both had legally changed their baptismal names and taken new ones that signified the life ahead of them rather than the life they'd left behind. Both were exceptional artists who preferred living alone and not talking about their personal lives. As such, it took several years for the two women to become devoted friends who accepted one another and didn't ask questions.

The painting in question, along with the two others, had been delivered by the artist herself. All three had been received and signed in by the lively, cheerful volunteers behind the desk. It was common knowledge that Rose would take at least one of the top three prizes. The only real question was which painting would get a ribbon and what color it would be. The three ladies on the intake desk, curious and a little intimidated by her energy and obsessive behavior, were in awe of the tiny woman's remarkable talent. Sometimes, they even took private bets on which of the turbulent, broad-stroked semi-abstractions would win. They found it surprising that she did such large and commanding work when she herself was so small and slight.

The ladies considered the three paintings: the fishing boat in the morning mist, the abstract snow-swept salt marsh, and the third, more disturbing painting—the one with two figures that could have been lovers or could just as easily have been warriors in battle. Each volunteer had an opinion on which would be the winner, and each of them wished—privately of course—that just once, someone else in the MAA would have a chance to take home the gold.

But at four o'clock in the afternoon, the winter-misted sun was setting fast, and those kinds of decisions were not theirs to make. It was time for the volunteers to go home. The following day, the missing painting would be located, the ladies would know which volunteer had the best eye, and the winner of their little wager would take the others out for a drink. And after the awards ceremony, Rose Doré would go home alone and add one more ribbon to her expanding collection.

Chapter Eight

❧❀❧

B y one o'clock in the afternoon, Pauline DeLaar—
chair of the board— her husband, Robert, the
gallery director, and Lynne Kostka, exhibit coordi-
nator, were standing around, waiting for the last judge to
show up. With them were three other members of the
governing board and two dedicated volunteers. A light
snow was falling intermittently outside, and they were
making meaningless small talk about the weather and the
condition of the roads when all six feet of Viridienne
Greene, snowflakes sparkling on her half-inch-long pewter
hair and on her ankle-length wool cape, came careening
through the rear door. She was totally out of breath and
carried a great lumpy package under her arm.

"Do I still have time to get my stuff in the show? I
mean, you haven't started judging yet, right? Of course
not, because there's only two of you, and I know for a fact
there are three judges."

Bob DeLaar shook his head and, without a word,

handed her a registration sheet and a pencil. He didn't even bother to remonstrate or resist. Viridienne coming in at the last minute was as predictable as Rose Doré arriving early and later taking one of the top prizes.

While she was filling out her papers, the rest of the board members and the volunteers were scurrying around, trying to get ready for the judging. They were setting up chairs, adjusting lights, and determining the order of the categories to be judged. But something was clearly amiss.

"Has anyone seen Rose Doré's third painting?" asked Pauline.

"What are you talking about? She brought them. I was here," said Lynne. "Three, as usual. Beautiful of course."

Pauline threw up her hands. "I can see two of them, but the third one's missing, and I can't find it. Do you think she might have put it somewhere else?"

Lynne shook her head, pointed at the wall by the door, and blinked. "That's where I saw them last. She doesn't want anything to be stacked against them, so she always puts them off to the side." She punctuated this explanation with a not-too-subtle eye roll.

"Well, you can see for yourself there are only two there now, and nothing's been touched since we locked up last night. I know—I was last one out and first one in this morning."

David Taylor, who had been silent, spoke up. "Jackson Smith came in to help set up this morning just as I arrived. When I saw there were only two, I asked him if he had any idea where it might be. He told me she'd called him and asked him to bring it to her. It was just like you said—she wanted to change something. She said she'd have it back here today in time for the judging."

"Who's Jackson Smith?" asked one of the newer volunteers.

"Oh, you know him. Glasses, short curly hair, kind of dark blond, not fat but a little on the stocky side. Old family. I think he's taken every class we offer." Lynne snickered and shook her head. "He's a god-awful artist, but bless his heart, he just loves it, and he keeps trying. You have to admire him for persistence if nothing else. I don't think he has much of a social life, and he likes being here. He's out now—said something about getting lunch. He'll be back later on. He never misses a judging. Worth his weight in gold, I'll tell you."

"Oh, sure, now I remember. I guess I didn't know his name." The new volunteer dropped her voice. "He can't have a regular job if he's here all the time. What's the story?"

"I think he has some kind of condition or disability or something. You don't just ask that kind of thing, do you? Anyway, it doesn't matter. He's certainly a help around here. I know for a fact that he volunteers at the animal shelter as well. I don't know what we'd do without him, especially when we're hanging a show. He's as strong as an ox. He should be back any minute. He's the one who always moves all the paintings around when we have a judging."

"Not only that, but he's one of our best customers," Pauline said.

"What do you mean?" the volunteer asked.

"He buys things all the time—paintings, photographs,

even sculptures. He must have a huge collection by now…
and he's a substantial donor. Like I said, old family and old
money." Pauline dropped her voice. "But don't repeat me."

"So he's got a few bucks?"

Pauline nodded. "Obviously, but it's not exactly something to discuss over a cup of coffee, now, is it? At least, I
wouldn't. And besides, who cares? It's his business,
not ours."

"So how does he get to be the one to transport her
paintings? We all know she's a fanatic about who touches
them." David was straightening and restraightening the
papers on the desk.

"He has a van, and she won't drive at night—or in any
kind of bad weather, for that matter. It's a win-win as far as
I'm concerned—which I'm not really, because it's none of
my business."

Lynne rolled her eyes. "He'd do it just to be helpful.
He's like that. But she insists on paying him. I think he
does a few odd jobs around the house for her as well. If she
said it's coming back, then it is… and if it doesn't come
back, we know who has it."

Viridienne spoke up. "Well, that makes sense. I've seen
her do this before—bring a painting in for a show only to
take it right back for one last final touch. We all know what
a perfectionist she is."

There were nods of agreement.

"The question is, then, why isn't it here now? That's *not*
like her. Did Jackson say when he'd be back?"

"No. The thing is, she might have simply changed her
mind and decided to hold that one out. She's done that

before too. What do you think, Viridienne? You know her better than we do."

Viridienne shook her head. "And that's not saying a whole lot. Tell you what—I'm finished here, so I'll swing by her house on my way home and see what's going on. That would be better than calling her. She'll have a total fit if she thinks we're checking up on her. She's so protective of her privacy."

"I wonder why?" David looked sadly perplexed.

Viridienne shrugged. "Hey, we all have stuff we don't talk about. It's not hurting anyone, and it's none of our business. I'll call you when I know what's going on… and for heaven's sake, call me if Jackson comes in with the painting."

Viridienne wrote her cell phone number on the back of a crumpled grocery-store receipt and handed it to Pauline. Then she unwrapped her own submissions: two richly textured vertical wall hangings, one of which would likely take another one of the top prizes. After placing them side by side on a long table, she swung her cape around her shoulders, hiked up the collar, and left through the rear door leading to the parking lot.

The light snow that had been spitting down all day was getting heavier. It would not be long before driving would be difficult. Viridienne was beginning to regret her impulsive offer to check on Rose, but the die had been cast—in more ways than one. Rose was her friend, and friends checked on friends.

Chapter Nine

Inside the gallery, the third judge had finally arrived, and all present were still in a total swivet, trying to decide what to do in the absence of the missing painting. They debated whether to proceed with the selection and the judging and deal with the fallout later or to wait to hear from Viridienne.

Pauline was about to make an executive decision when the front door opened. "Well, look who's here…and look what he's carrying. Hallelujah! The lost is found."

Jackson Smith attempted to smile a greeting over his shoulder as he backed in through the door. He was carrying the painting, protectively covered in snow-spotted plastic trash bags, all the while apologizing for his late return.

"Problem solved," said Pauline. "Guess there was a mix-up and somebody forgot to call somebody. Wouldn't be the first time that's happened around this place, would it? The important thing is that they're here. Thank God! Just put it over there, will you, Jackson?" She pointed assertively. "No, a little more to the left. Against the wall where nothing else will touch it. Now, then, with everything present and accounted for, I guess we can get started. You're staying for the judging, aren't you? We really need an extra pair of hands."

Jackson nodded. "That was my plan. You know me—I like to help. I had a couple of errands to run after I picked up the artwork from Rose, and the driving's getting worse. It took me a lot longer than I thought to finally get here." He'd pulled off his coat and was carefully rolling up his sleeves. "Show me where to start."

For the next two hours, the volunteers moved painting after painting as the three judges—two men and a woman —walked through the different categories of artwork, pausing here and there. The multimedia open show had a little bit of everything to choose from, and anyone who was a member could submit up to three paintings. The entries went from garishly painted children with big eyes to any number of sand-swept dune scenes and abandoned farm trucks. The more original, cut-above-the-others pieces included two pure abstracts, a watercolor seascape by a noted local, Viridienne's wall hangings, and the three stunning paintings by Rose Doré. Everyone was admiring the paintings when a screeching siren coming from the direction of the main road interrupted their conversation.

Robert Kostka shook his head. "This is no time to be out on the roads. It's getting dark, and the snow is picking up. New Englanders should know better." He turned to the others. "I say we either hurry up and get finished with this or stop now and come back tomorrow when the driving's better. I'd hate to have any of us get hurt. It's not like judging an art show is a life-or-death situation or anything. The paintings aren't going anywhere."

Avery Smith, one of the judges, responded. "We're here now. The main roads are usually okay. It's coming down harder now, but the sanding trucks are already out. I say we get this show on the road... so to speak."

"Oh, crap," said Robert. "I totally forgot to call Viridienne and tell her the painting is here."

"Well, she never called us either," said Lynne. "So I guess no news is good news. She knows how to put two and two together as well as we do. I'm sure Rose told her what happened, and she went home. End of story."

And so they continued on until the winners and runners-up were discussed and selected and the ribbons of many colors were affixed to the lucky few.

"I think this calls for a drink," said Vaughn Keller, another of the volunteers. "We can walk up the street and try out that new place, the Dog and Whistle."

"You mean the one that's trying to be an English pub?"

"I do indeed. They're doing a pretty good job, and despite all of the attempts at British authenticity, they've at least been persuaded to serve the beer cold."

This produced some gentle laughter.

Jackson was looking doubtful. "You can count me out. By the sound of that siren earlier, there has been at least one accident tonight. I don't think I want to be the next one. I'm going home to hang out with my dogs. Guess I'll see you all tomorrow. I'll get here early, though. That way, I can get some salt and sand on the steps."

"I'll second that," said Vaughn.

Reluctantly, they all agreed that it was better to be safe than sorry, and they called it a day. They would have a drink together another time—maybe after the awards party. The more immediate plan was to hold off hanging the paintings until the following day, when the roads were clear.

"Sounds like a plan," said Pauline. "I have all of your numbers. If there's any kind of change, I'll do a call around. And Jackson, how about I give you an hour's head start?"

"Works for me," said Jackson.

"Okay, then, everybody—out of here. I'll lock up," Pauline said.

Her husband mock saluted and made a great show of running for the door.

Chapter Ten

❦

I t had been done quickly and efficiently. All had gone according to plan, and she'd never seen it coming. His strategy and practice had paid off. Of course, he would have preferred not to kill her, but when all was said and done, she'd given him no choice. She'd been warned—more than once. Maybe she thought it was all behind them and long forgotten. Well, it wasn't. With one well-practiced blow to the back of the head, it was over. Once she was down, he'd turned her over and added the smear of red paint across her mouth, more as an exclamation point than a desecration of her body—a visual *The End* to a modern-day Greek tragedy. His tragedy. *And hers.*

Back outside and on the street, he hunched down into his jacket, crammed his fists into his pockets, and walked back to his car. Once inside, he sat curled into himself, waiting for the heat to come on. He was badly chilled and needed to warm up and stop shaking before he could drive. *All over but the shouting,* he thought, remembering another of his grandfather's oft-repeated sayings. *But will it be over? Will ending her life put an end to the lifelong agony, this love-hate relationship?*

She should have been my wife. The man slammed his bare fist against the ice-cold steering wheel and immediately wished he hadn't. He waited for the pain in his fingers to subside before starting the car and pulling away from the curb.

In flight mode, he rode the crest of his adrenaline surge, yet he was fully aware that the inevitable crash to earth was going to be tsunamic, a wave that would wash over him and bury him for weeks. *Is it finally over? And if so, now what?*

He'd lost her so many years before. So why was he crying? He should have felt relief—the debt had been paid. Never again would he be forced to see her with another man... or another woman. *Jesus, not that!*

In the days leading up to this, he'd often seen her hanging out with that weird-looking artist friend of hers, Viridienne Greene. *What kind of a made-up stage name is that? And is she even a woman?* As he thought about her buzz cut, basketball-player build, and face like a horse, he really wasn't sure what Viridienne was, but he hated her as well. He hated anyone Rose might have looked on with favor. The very thought of them together turned his stomach. It had taken him some time to find out the woman's name— or the name she went by—but if nothing else, he had time. Anyone—man or woman—who spent time with his beloved Xenia was a threat. He'd think about Viridienne later. At the moment, shaking as badly as he was and with the snow picking up, it took everything he had to keep the car on the road.

He realized it had been hours since he'd eaten, but the thought of food turned his stomach to the point where he thought he might have to pull over and throw up. And that brought up even more terrors. He couldn't stop on the side of the road or do anything that might attract police attention. He swallowed hard, gripped the wheel with both hands, and drove on.

Chapter Eleven

As she made her way along the snowy streets, Viridienne thought about Rose living alone all these years in an eleven-room rambling Victorian mansion overlooking Plymouth Harbor. It was one of the few houses from that era that had remained untouched and had not been converted into rental units, or worse, repurposed and modernized as condominiums. How Rose had come to own it was another of her private mysteries. Viridienne had visited any number of times, usually on association business or for private-studio showings. The whole first floor had been made into a kind of public-gallery sitting-room area to display her artwork and occasionally entertain clients and patrons.

The working studio, her living quarters, private sitting room, and several bedrooms were upstairs on the second floor. The top floor was an unheated attic no doubt used for servants' quarters when the house was built. Rose kept it locked and made little reference to it. Viridienne had seen it only once, when Rose had taken her up there to show her the paintings she'd done that no one in Plymouth would ever see. Rose let her have one look then locked the door again. She knew that if Rose intended for her to know more about those paintings and why they were hidden away, she would tell her. She knew better than to ask.

As much as Viridienne loved the privacy and isolation of her little cottage, in weather like this, the idea of a rented room that was easier to heat and right in the center of town would be of considerable advantage. At one point she'd even thought about asking Rose if she might consider letting her rent some space in one of the attic rooms. She'd thought about it but she'd never actually spoken the words out loud. The attic and its contents were locked away. Off limits.

But with the snow swirling around her car she considered the possibility of bringing it up that night. The idea of firing up the woodstove in her tiny drafty house on the pond underlined the necessity of at least asking the question. She shivered at the thought of going home to the chilly cottage. *Not a year-round rental*, she mused, *but just maybe one or two months in the winter or even as a pied-à-terre for occasional personal use.* Deuteronomy had already given Rose the paws-up of approval, and he was an excellent judge of character. If he sat on your lap of his own free will, you were his friend for life. If he didn't like you, he would sit guard beside Viridienne and glower. But most telling of all, if he really took against you, he would pee on an article of your clothing. His judgment was unerring. When DT peed, Viridienne took heed.

She moved carefully along the snow-covered streets, thinking about Rose's enormous house. It would be nice to be able have a place like that and not have to worry about money. But she'd long since decided that it wasn't worth what it would take to achieve the national recognition that would produce that kind of lifestyle. She could never play the art game the way she would have to in order to claw her way to the top in a big city. Like Rose, but for very different reasons, she chose to stay in Plymouth and bloom where she had planted herself. Rather than seek national recognition at a cost she couldn't bring herself to pay, she would live on less and be able to look at herself in the mirror, happy with what she saw.

Her little reverie was sharply interrupted when she skidded as she signaled and turned her disreputable Volvo wagon into Rose's cobbled driveway. The skid startled her. Viridienne took personal pride in being a good driver—especially as a transplanted New Englander driving in the snow. She squinted and peered out of the window. There was not too much accumulated yet, but the roads looked slippery as hell nonetheless. She pulled up beside her friend's car and parked under the huge oak tree that stood guardian over the house. With its leaves gone, it looked skeletal and menacing. Still, bare as it was, it would deflect some of the falling snow. Viridienne turned off the engine, looked up at the big old house, and smiled. The lights were on, which meant her friend was home. *Good!* Hopefully, there'd be time for a cup of coffee or tea—a quick warm-up before the drive home.

She walked up the front steps, squeaked across the snow-covered porch, and rang the bell. The faint sound of music came from inside the house. She rang again, listening hard for approaching footsteps or the sound of a creaking floorboard. Nothing. She knocked and tried the handle and was surprised to find the door unlocked. Viridienne frowned in sudden, unexpected concern. Rose didn't go out and leave lights on, and even if she was home, she never left the door unlocked. Besides, her car was in the driveway. Viridienne had parked her own car behind it.

She pushed open the door and stepped inside. "Rose? Rose, you home? It's me, Viridienne."

Now that she was inside, the music was louder. She pulled off her snow-spotted cape and dropped it on a chair. Then, with growing discomfort, she followed the sound to the foot of the wide, curved stairway that led to Rose's spacious studio on the floor above. The familiar smells of oil paint, linseed oil, and varnish comingled with herb-scented potpourri and musty old-house smells, bringing back fragments of vague, dusty memories of her own childhood. She shook her head and brushed them away like late-summer yellow jackets—ready to sting if they got too close but harmless as long as they didn't land on her.

"Rose?" she called again more tentatively. "Rose? You up there?" She was less than halfway up the stairs when she knew for certain that something was very, very wrong. She detected another smell—faint, like the music, and also familiar. A smell that she associated with shame and humiliation. She stopped, counted to ten, and made her way slowly to the top of the stairs.

The door of the studio was slightly ajar. Viridienne called out once again as she pushed it open then grabbed the doorknob to keep from losing her balance. Her best friend lay twisted and motionless on the floor.

In death—and there was no question that she was dead —Rose Doré seemed even smaller than she had in life. She looked like a crumpled paper doll. Her pale unseeing eyes, still wide in a rictus of terror and shock, stared up at the ceiling. There was a pool of dried blood under her head and shoulders... and perhaps most distressing of all, a vicious smear of red paint slashed across the face and open mouth of the woman lying on the floor. The brush, still wet and laden with the red paint, lay next to her.

ON THE OTHER SIDE OF TOWN, INSIDE THE GALLERY, Jackson Smith remained behind the others in order to turn off the lights and turn down the heat. There would be more than usual to do the next day because of the storm, and he planned to arrive early to help. The volunteers would have to mount the exhibition and, at the same time, get ready for the opening reception scheduled for later that day. Chaos. Still, by the looks of it, it was going to be a beautiful show. He smiled into the darkened and rapidly cooling space then pulled the door shut behind him and stepped out into the snow.

Chapter Twelve

Viridienne didn't scream. Too shaken to make a sound and hanging onto the doorknob to keep herself from collapsing, she stood frozen in horror, looking at the scene before her. When she was sure her legs wouldn't give way, Viridienne turned and, with both hands clamped onto the railing, crept down the stairs to the ground floor. She dropped into the nearest chair and, using Rose's house phone, called 911.

Then, summoning her last vestige of strength, she called the main number of the MAA, only to have the call picked up by the answering machine. She thought about leaving a message saying only that there was a problem and they should get on with the judging. But the words would not come. Viridienne looked at the phone in her hand, shook her head, and slowly returned it to the stand. She sat and waited, numb with shock, until she heard the sirens getting louder and louder as they approached the house.

Now what do I do?

Viridienne didn't have an answer for that. She pulled back her sleeve to look at her watch and realized she was shaking all over. When she'd seen this stuff on TV and read about it in books, they'd called it fiction, only this wasn't fiction. The siren cut off mid howl, and the flashing lights flickered against the far wall as the police car and the ambulance pulled up outside the house.

Still wobbly, she walked to the door to let them in. "Up there." She turned and indicated the staircase behind her.

The two paramedics, along with a uniformed police officer, ran in and clanked upstairs with all their gear. Viridienne stayed and waited in the sitting room with two more police officers—a youngish man whose name tag identified him as DI Fitzpatrick and a woman, DI Alison Grey. Still too shaken to talk, she was trying not to hear the noises coming from the room at the top of the stairs, sounds of living people moving softly around a person who was not living. Her friend Rose was up there, lying on the floor, brutally murdered. She heard men and women doing their grisly job, cameras clicking, and the soft grunt as people lifted a body and placed it onto a stretcher. She tried not to hear the rasping of a full-length zipper being pulled one way and then, a few minutes later, the sound repeated, more muffled this time. And then she heard the descent. They were bringing Rose down. Viridienne wanted to look away but found she couldn't. She stood and waited—no leg wobbles this time. The EMTs wheeled the shrouded body past her. The attending officer held the door open to let them pass. Viridienne, followed, head bowed, walking slowly beside her friend. She stood in the blowing snow while they collapsed the gurney and slid it and its forlorn little burden into the medical examiner's van.

"You'd better get inside, miss. It's really cold out, and you don't have a coat on. You're gonna get wet and frozen." Fitzpatrick grabbed the blanket that was strapped to the end of the gurney, shook it open, and dropped it around her shoulders. After the ambulance pulled away, he and Alison Grey steered her back toward the light and warmth of the empty house.

Not used to having someone else look out for her, she was caught off guard by the unexpected kindness. She was freezing and found the gesture of comfort welcome and reassuring. When they were inside, Alison closed the door and asked Viridienne if, as the person who'd discovered the body and made the 911 call, she would stay and give them some basic information about the deceased.

"Could you help us with names of the next of kin and how to get in touch with them?"

By way of saying yes, Viridienne nodded and dropped back into the chair she'd sat in earlier. She was chilled and asked DI Grey for her cape, which was still crumpled on the chair in the hallway. Alison fetched the cape and offered to get her some water or even, if she could find her way around the kitchen, make her a cup of tea. Viridienne said yes to the water.

"Who should we notify?" asked the man named Fitzpatrick.

"There is no next of kin…" said Viridienne in a flat voice. "At least, not that she ever talked about. I probably knew her as well as anyone here in Plymouth, and I have to tell you, Rose Doré was a very private person. Any mention of family and relatives was off limits. She was interested in art, and she liked ethnic cooking. Greek food was her specialty. But parents, brothers, sisters ..." She shook her head in sad frustration. "Of course, she had a family, but she never talked about them. It was a closed subject. I do know this much: her real name was Xenia Stamos, and she grew up in Rhode Island.

Detective Fitzpatrick was scribbling notes but stopped and looked up. "Wouldn't you say that was a bit strange? A family that close and no contact?"

Viridienne nodded sadly. "Rose was more than a little bit strange, Detective. It's like she had no life before moving into this house. I learned to accept it. I'll tell you, though, she was one hell of an artist. We all wondered why she came here to Plymouth of all places, but like so much else about her, we learned not to ask."

"But she was your friend. You're the one who found her. You were used to coming into her house. Did she make a habit of leaving the door open?" He frowned and started writing again.

"We had each other's keys, but I only used her key when she wasn't home. We would often check on each other's houses if either of us was away. It was only when I saw the lights on and she didn't answer the bell or my banging on the door that I became concerned and took out my key..." She gulped. "But obviously, I didn't need it. The door was open. I mean, it was closed, but it wasn't locked."

Viridienne wondered whether or not she was making any sense. She didn't feel as if she was. Nothing was making any sense at the moment. She knew a fair amount about Rose's backstory, but it had been told to her in the strictest confidence late one night after one too many glasses of wine.

Murder did change the rules—Viridienne knew that—but if Rose wanted her past kept a secret, then Viridienne, even in her shaken state, owed her that one loyalty. If at some point in the future she felt it would help someone find Rose's killer, she would of course supply what information she could, but that would be her decision. For the time being, she would tell the police what little she knew that was considered public information—which was not much and could likely be found at Town Hall. Rose was a registered voter, had a driver's license, and owned a massive house, so she paid taxes and water bills—statistics, really, but it was a place to start. She'd told them Rose's real name and the fact that she'd grown up in Rhode Island. Nowadays, with Google and Ancestry and everything else on the Internet, it wouldn't be too hard for them to find someone to notify.

When Viridienne finished telling them what she felt she could, Detective Fitzpatrick thanked her, gave her his card, and asked her to get in touch with him if anything else came to mind. He also said it might be necessary for her to come in to the station and tell what she knew to the people assigned to investigating the case.

Their official duties done, Alison collected her things and told Fitzpatrick she'd go warm up the cruiser. He thanked her and began assembling his own things but stopped at the door. "What about you, miss? This is a crime scene. You need to leave as well. I need to lock up and secure the house. The forensics team will come back tomorrow. Uh, you didn't touch anything or move anything did you?"

Viridienne shook her head. "Other than the doorknobs and the railing on the stairs... and the telephone of course." She didn't want to ask the next question, but she had to know. She cleared her throat. "Umm, did they say how long she's been dead?"

"The medical examiner will be able to fix a more precise time, but off the top of my head, I'd say five or six hours. Rigor was setting in." He changed the subject. "Do you have a way to get home? You should probably get going. The roads are getting pretty bad. Do you need a ride?"

Viridienne shook her head. "My car's in the driveway."

"That old Volvo out there?"

Again she nodded. "It's old, it creaks and rattles, and it's drafty, just like my little old house, but it gets me where I need to go. I'll be all right. I've lived in New England long enough to almost be considered a native. I can manage."

"Agreed, miss, but you've also had one hell of a shock tonight. Do you think you should be alone? Is there someone you can call?"

"I have a cat and a spider plant."

"I'm not joking." He scowled at her.

"I'm not joking either. I'm a lot like Rose. Maybe that's why we became such good friends. Neither of us had family. All we had was the art. At least I have a cat I can go home to. If you don't have anything, you can't lose anything, can you?"

Viridienne swung her heavy cape over her, double

wrapped the scarf ties around her neck, and began pulling on her gloves while Fitzpatrick went around turning off lights and turning down the heat. "Shouldn't you leave a couple on just for safety's sake—I mean so the house doesn't look empty?" she asked.

The officer smiled a little sadly. "The yellow tape and the evening news are going to make everything public. But yes, we'll leave the hall light on. Come on—I'll walk you to your car. But if you change your mind about staying alone, call the station house, and we'll come get you and bring you to a hotel or a B and B here in town."

"Thanks, Officer. I'll be okay."

"Where do you live?"

"Out near the State Forest on Skye Pond. I live in a converted summer cottage. It's not much, but the price was right. It's all main roads until you get to the one I live on, then it's dirt, stones, and ruts all the way to my house."

He nodded. "You have my card. I want you to call in to HQ when you get home. Okay?"

"Okay." Viridienne wasn't used to someone looking out for her safety, and she didn't know what to do with it. "Thank you, Officer."

"Just drive slow, okay? And watch out for black ice."

THE SNOW WAS COMING DOWN MORE HEAVILY, AND THE wind was picking up. It was not going to be fit for man or beast out there before long. And somewhere in all that cold and lovely whiteness was a killer with a black heart who had Rose Doré's blood and streaks of red paint on his hands.

If Rose had been dead for several hours before she'd been found, the killer had plenty of time to get away before the roads got bad, and the falling snow would have covered up any footprints. Viridienne knew in her heart it had to have been a man. No woman in her right mind could have done that. But she couldn't think who would have done it and why. Rose was far too private to have made any enemies who hated her enough to kill her. On the other hand, maybe that was why she was so private. She had a past she kept locked up. Maybe it got loose and caught up with her.

Viridienne shook her head in dismay and applied a gentle, even pressure to the gas pedal. The night that they'd both had too much to drink and told each other their secrets, Viridienne learned some of the reasons Rose lived in Plymouth and why she was so private. She shook her head and wondered if she'd ever find out the whole truth. *I do know one thing, though*—she pushed the key into the lock of her cottage door and gave it a savage twist—*I'm damn sure going to try.*

Xenia hadn't told her everything about her tortured past, but she'd said enough for Viridienne to know it was ugly. Viridienne knew where to start looking if she or anyone else was going to find out the truth about why Rose had died and who'd killed her. As she considered her next course of action, she could hear Old Deuteronomy on the other side of the door. He was hungry.

Chapter Thirteen

❧

Once inside the cottage, Viridienne dropped her wet things on the bench beside the door and made straight for the woodstove to fire it up. The cat was voicing his own needs at an ever-increasing volume, but first things first—they needed heat. She always set the space heater to fifty-five before she went out, to keep the house from freezing.

In minutes, she had a nice fire going in the woodstove, and within minutes after that, she'd set a dish of fresh evil-smelling food on the floor by the back door.

Slinging rough-cut logs around allowed Viridienne to release the crippling tension in her neck and shoulders. *Heat first, food for the noisy beastie next.*

Old Deuteronomy was a one-eyed burnt orange Maine coon cat she'd rescued from the gas chamber only weeks after she moved to Plymouth. Because of his size—he weighed over twenty pounds—and his partial blindness, he was considered unadoptable and was scheduled to be euthanized the day she visited the shelter. She'd taken one look at that beautiful, frightened animal and started filling out the papers. That they'd found each other exactly when they had was way beyond coincidence and almost predestination. Viridienne was virulently antireligious, but in quiet moments, she considered the thought that if divine intervention existed, the fact that she and Old Deuteronomy had found each other exactly when they had came pretty damn close to it.

The fiber artist and the one-eyed cat were a good match. They both liked their creature comforts—good food, a glowing fire in the woodstove, and a ready lap. DT, as she nicknamed him, kept her little cottage free of anything with tiny little feet, skinny tails, and whiskers. He'd miraculously adjusted to being an indoor cat in the time it took to learn his name. Coyotes and coywolves were becoming more and more prevalent in the woods that surrounded her Jack-built house, and with only one eye, DT wouldn't have stood a chance as an outdoor cat.

With a full glass of wine in one hand and a steaming cup of herb tea in the other, Viridienne was ready to collapse. Outside, the storm was in full force, but it was no match for the emotional storm whirling around inside her mind. Once settled, with her feet up on the antique footstool she'd picked up on one of her thrift-shop adventures, she pulled out her cell phone, called police headquarters, and asked for DI Fitzpatrick. He was not available so, as directed, she left a message on his voicemail saying she was home safe and sound and thanking him for his help and support earlier that evening. With that last piece of practicality of the way, she pushed away the tea, took a large swallow of her wine, set her glass down on the table beside her, and broke into the gut-wrenching sobs she'd been holding in since the awful moment when she'd found her friend on the floor.

She fully gave herself over to grief and outrage. The idea that someone would forever stop the heart and hand of that talented, wonderful woman was beyond comprehension. Her next broken thought was to wonder what in the world would drive a person to do such a horrid thing to another human being. It was too much to take in.

DT, ever sensitive to her moods, abandoned his food and heaved himself up onto her lap. The food could wait. He had a job to do.

Eventually, Viridienne wiped her eyes, blew her nose into the soggy Kleenex she held crumpled in one hand and with her free hand, she stroked the cat. She thought back to the night when she and Rose told each other their secrets. Both were survivors—escapees from violence and tyranny, one religious and one domestic, each of them utterly dehumanizing to a creative soul.

Viridienne told Rose all about her life as Obedient Charity. How in order to survive, she had to walk away from everything and everyone she knew and loved forever. She even admitted to the lingering sadness and guilt over abandoning Thankful, the vulnerable little sister she'd left behind. She went on to tell the story of how, in the days after she left the compound, she became Viridienne Greene and eventually settled into being the quirky, solitary fiber artist that Rose knew.

And then, after they'd opened another bottle of wine, Rose Doré told her story. She'd been born Xenia Stamos, a first-generation Greek American. She was the oldest of four children whose hardworking immigrant parents were strict and fiercely protective of their only daughter—and absolutely devastated when she announced that she wanted to go to art school. A woman's job was to be a wife and a mother and stay in the neighborhood so she could look after her parents as they aged. They asked themselves and her three brothers where they had failed and what they had done to deserve this.

Xenia persisted and eventually got her way but only if she agreed to live at home and commute daily to the Rhode Island School of Design, one of the most prestigious art colleges in the country. Her talent was such that after the first year, she was given a full scholarship, and by her junior year, she was selling her paintings and working a few hours a week in a local art gallery. It was also in her junior year that she ran into Nicolo Brandosi. He, too, was a painting major and was much wiser in the ways of women than she was in the ways of men. He moved in on her like a wolf stalking its prey, sweeping her off her feet and into his bed within weeks of their meeting. In a few months' time, shortly after Christmas of that same year, he pressed her into a town-hall marriage with only his brother present as a witness.

"Until death do you part," said the clerk at the end of the three-minute ceremony.

And they both said, "I will."

Once they were married, day by relentless day, Nicolo slowly took over her life and her art. The man was no fool —he'd recognized her extraordinary talent and knew that he'd never come anywhere close to being as good as she was. The only way he could attain the recognition he wanted for himself was to exercise complete control over his beautiful, dutiful, "love, honor, and obey" new wife and see that her paintings, as well as her body, belonged only to him.

Her distraught parents eventually got over the shock of the hasty marriage. As the days passed and they finally ascertained that she wasn't pregnant—their worst nightmare—their outrage slowly morphed into polite surface-only acceptance of the situation. But they never really trusted him. He'd robbed them of a daughter and the chance to have a lavish wedding, and although they didn't know it at the time, he would also deny them the blessing of grandchildren.

Chapter Fourteen

Viridienne shivered. The house was warm but drafty. The persistent wind outside had plenty of places to gain entrance. One more thing to write on her bucket list: find and block drafts.

"But that's a project for warmer weather, DT. Just remind me, okay?" The cat nodded in her direction. Like many people who lived alone, she often had extended conversations with her cat or, if he wasn't interested, with herself.

She pushed a fresh log into the stove and pulled a shawl out of a tangled pile of almost-finished projects in her knitting basket. Promising herself, once again, to weave in the loose ends one of these days, she wrapped its delicate comfort around her shoulders and curled herself back down into her chair.

"Now, where was I?" she asked the cat and once again sank into the muddled memories and stories surrounding her dead friend.

The artistic takeover of Xenia Stamos started off innocently enough right after she and Nicolo were married. He had an assignment due the following day and told her he'd run out of time. He asked if she would just finish it up for him. "Just a splash here and there, and maybe clean up the edges a little."

Certainly, as a good wife, she could do that for him. After that, he relentlessly and methodically pressed her for more and more of her time and talent until eventually, she was doing all of his work while her own work went into a marked and rapid decline. Up until their marriage, his work was seen as highly skilled but derivative and often overworked. Xenia's early work was luminous, powerful, and almost otherworldly in its subject matter and technique. But before long, she and her art began to change. In the beginning, her professors didn't see what was happening, and when they finally did, nobody took the time to address it with her. They simply shrugged and turned away. After the marriage, she began to lose interest in her work, and within months of the wedding, she resigned her teaching-assistant job, saying she was needed at home. At the end of her junior year, with no clear reason or advance warning, she withdrew completely from RISD and went home to be a wife to her husband.

It was too bad, her teachers said, but they'd seen it happen before. Women, even if they had the talent—"and God knows, this one did"—too often let it fall away once they were married and found themselves with a house and husband to look after. It was the way of the world. They shook their collective heads and asked no more questions. There would be other promising students.

Only it wasn't the way of the world. Xenia had slowly become a slave to her husband's jealousy and ambition. Subject to physical and emotional abuse if she dared challenge him in any way, she faded into the background and more and more remained hidden away in her studio, where she was able to lose herself and her misery in her painting while he collected the fame, glory, and money. She signed his name on every one, and with each one she completed, she gave away a little more of herself. He collected the commissions and posed for the news photographs and granted the interviews. Xenia, when summoned, made brief appearances, served drinks, and was lovingly introduced as the "power behind the artist." She came when called, spoke when spoken to, was available for sex anytime, anywhere… and any kind, no matter how brutal and degrading. Above all, she had to keep those paintings coming… or else.

She tried once to run away from him. It was weeks before the bruises healed and she was able to go out in public. But in that short burst of freedom, she'd seen the light. Several months later, on a night when Nicolo was being fawned over at yet another press-filled gallery opening and she knew he would not be home until well after midnight, she called her younger brother, Yanni. Then, with nothing more than the clothes she was wearing, she left for good. Not even her parents knew about the escape. She would tell them, of course, but not yet. She was too broken. In her family, no matter who you married or how bad it was, divorce was a sin and an unthinkable disgrace. But Xenia knew that if life was a living hell on earth, what might come in the hereafter could be no worse. She needed time alone to heal in the safety and protection of the one person in the world she trusted. Though the Brandosis would be cunning and vindictive in trying to reclaim their most prized possession, Yanni Stamos—Xenia's fiercely protective younger brother—was better than any of them at protecting his own.

Two months after Xenia had left Nicolo, he was found dead in their Jacuzzi. His family hinted to police that Xenia might have had something to do with it and tried to press charges. But there was no sign of foul play, and eventually, it was determined that he'd most likely overdosed on alcohol and pills then slipped, hit his head, and drowned. The newspapers reported it as an unfortunate accident, but everyone connected to it knew it was not the end of the story. More than a few questions were left unanswered. They were like mold, collecting and festering in the dark places.

The art journals called Nicolo's death the tragedy of the century. At the time of the inquest, Xenia told them she was unaware that he'd been involved with drugs, but there was so much about him she didn't know that this latest came as no surprise. She didn't tell the investigators about the constant abuse or who had really been doing those spectacular paintings, because they didn't ask. They did ask if he had been under any particular or unusual stress of late.

She shrugged. "Who knows? He didn't talk about anything personal."

"Were you and Nicolo having marital problems?" they asked her.

"No more than any other couple."

"Was he seeing someone else? "

"I'd be the last to know. It's not exactly something you discuss with your wife, is it?"

And then, without warning, came the grab-and-go question. "So did you kill him?"

"No."

"Why aren't you more emotional? You just lost your husband. Life is going to be very different for you. Aren't you going to miss him?"

"We were married, but we lived in different worlds."

"What is that supposed to mean?"

"He was out working in the world, and I stayed at home. Very traditional arrangement."

"You said 'arrangement' and not marriage. Were you married or weren't you?"

"I was married all right."

"You are not being very helpful."

"In some ways, he was a total stranger. He was not the man I fell in love with."

"So you did have problems, but you stayed with him until you left him, and then a few weeks later, he's found dead in the bathtub. Supposedly of an overdose."

"Okay, we had problems," she said. "He was getting more moody and more violent. I was afraid of him. Now that I think of it, I suppose that could have been because of the drugs, right?"

"You left him because you were afraid of him, but you didn't kill him."

"That's right."

"Is there anything else you might be able to tell us that

would help us understand some of the factors leading up to his death?

"No, not really… not right now, anyway. I'm pretty out of it at the moment. This whole thing's been a nightmare."

But the nightmare was still a work in progress. Xenia, the young widow, would soon learn that everything she thought that she and Nicolo owned in common—the money, stock interests, and rights and residuals to all of her paintings—had been put into an irrevocable trust with his family named as the trustees. She was a penniless black-swathed widow… but she was alive, and she was free of his unrelenting tyranny. Above all, inside and underneath the black clothing and bruised heart, she was an artist. It would take some time to reclaim that part of her, but it was the one thing he could not beat out of her.

Eventually, after the murder, the speculation and gossip faded out of the news cycle. Xenia stayed on with her brother, slowly moving back into her own body and healing, until the night the Brandosi family lawyer called and asked to meet with her, alone, at a popular restaurant in downtown Providence. There, with the noise and clatter of a busy restaurant serving as a curtain of white sound, he outlined the conditions of her future and the future safety of her immediate family.

The terms were unequivocal. She was to guarantee complete and complicit silence about the real source of Nicolo's paintings. She would move away, change her identity, and continue to produce the paintings. She would sign his name and keep the paintings hidden away until such time as a representative of the Brandosi family would call and collect them. Then they would be exhibited and sold as "recently discovered Brandosi masterpieces," with the broad hint that there were likely to be several more—if not hundreds more—out there, waiting to be found. Brandosi was a prolific painter—everybody who knew him knew that.

"And isn't it strange," they said a little too often and a little too loudly, "that his silly little mouse of a wife—what was her name again?—just up and disappeared after everything was said and done? Wonder where she went off to? What does that tell you? If you ask me, she got away with murder. Never mind. We've still got the paintings. She'll get hers in the end. They always do."

The terms of agreement were unalterable. Xenia would change her name and never display any of her own work in public again. She would move to another state where they would buy and give her full title to a house of her choice, where she would continue to make paintings that would be "discovered" over time. In exchange for this, they would provide her with a comfortable income for life and the solemn promise that nothing bad would ever happen to any members of her family. They had *connections*, he told her, and would take care of all the legal arrangements and expenses and arrange for the transition. They would keep the existing paintings and sell them off for the fortune they were worth. The care and feeding of the woman who'd created them was chump change compared to the money they would bring in.

The Brandosi lawyer and spokesman made it clear that if she violated the terms of the contract—if she ever told the truth about the paintings—she and any friend or family member she had spoken to would disappear. If she kept to the terms, then all further connections with the Brandosi family would be permanently severed, and she would be free to go. It wasn't really a choice, and at that point, she didn't care. She'd been captive for too long, and anything, even the loss of her art, was worth the price of once again having a life and keeping her family safe. Her family, even at a distance, was all she had. After years of isolation, she had no friends.

In the following weeks, Xenia found herself a big old house in Plymouth with an ocean view from the second floor and near enough to the center of town to be within walking distance to everything but not so near that she would be bothered by noise and street traffic. It was also a little over an hour to Providence but still far enough away that she was not likely to be recognized by a neighbor or an old schoolmate if she walked down the street for a cup of coffee.

She changed her name, signed on the dotted line, and began a new life as Rose Doré, her favorite color. It was warm, vibrant, thick pink-crimson, a symbol of the self she'd lost and the self she would one day recover. Not too long after that, purely by chance, while visiting a local art and craft show, she made the acquaintance of Viridienne Greene, a rangy long-legged silver-haired fiber artist with a backstory as desperate and bizarre as her own. The two women had taken a long and cautious time to dare to become friends, but it was well worth the wait.

Viridienne wiped away a leftover tear. Her one true friend was gone. So much was gone now. DT reached up and, in the mindreading way of cats, touched Viridienne's cheek with his paw. She'd endured losses before, and she could do it again. *But a friend like Rose? Warm, vibrant Rose...*

"Thanks, my fuzzy little cockeyed friend. I guess it's just you and me against the world now."

By way of response, DT blinked his one good eye at her and curled against her chest and stomach, letting his bone-rattling purr be a comfort to the pair of them. Viridienne leaned back, wrapped her arms around the vibrating animal, and closed her eyes.

Chapter Fifteen

❧❀❧

The man was home, picking at a Chinese takeout. Food was fodder, something to fill the hole, a bodily requirement. He could go for days on peanut butter and jelly, but that night, he wanted more. He was ravenous, and he didn't cook.

His one luxury and sensual pleasure was real coffee. Dark, strong, freshly ground when possible, and none of those pussy-assed flavors like hazelnut or—God forbid—Irish cream. A good cup of fresh coffee and a double shot of really fine scotch, straight up, with a couple of drops of water to open the flavor—those were two of his very few self-indulgences.

The food had been a mistake. He went out into the kitchen, dropped the half-full paper plate into the wastebasket, and reached into the cupboard for his bottle of Scotch. He carried the bottle, a glass, and a cup of water back into the living room where, seated in front of the TV, he poured himself a double and turned on the evening news. He sipped and stared at the flickering screen, hoping to settle his racing thoughts, but he was too wired to know what he was looking at. This thing had been years in the planning. All his life, he'd gotten the short end of the stick, the smaller cookie, and the second choice when it came to women. Well, fuck them. This time, he'd gotten the last word. Too bad there was nobody left to tell—nobody whose nose he could rub in the shit he'd been dealt all his life. Nobody to share a drink or a cigarette with.

He was finally beginning to grasp that it was over and that, after all that time spent in the shadows, he'd finally come out on top and declared himself the winner. But he felt so empty. That was an unwelcome surprise. He chewed on the corner of a familiar fingernail and considered the wisdom of having another measure of scotch. He wasn't much of a drinker—never had been. Still, if he was ever going to get some sleep... he drained what was left in the glass and reached for the bottle.

Chapter Sixteen

On the other side of the country, in the secretive Society of Obedient Believers, Obedient Thankful was plotting her escape. It seemed like forever since the night Charity had left the Society of Obedient Believers. In all that time, Thankful had never stopped thinking about her beloved sister and protector. The rules of the community strictly forbade her to speak of one who had left, so Thankful kept the image of her sister's face and the feel of her capable hands locked away with the scrap of paper she'd found in her jacket pocket. Even though she'd memorized the words, the actual sight and feel of her sister's handwriting comforted her.

Sometimes, she'd linger in her room, sitting on the edge of the bed and running her fingers over the words that had faded until they were virtually illegible. One day she would do the same—break free. It was a question of when and, of course, how. As with her sister, life beyond the walls meant freedom and survival. She felt as if she was dying on the inside and the outside.

Thankful carefully refolded the scrap of paper and tucked it back into its hiding place. She didn't have much time left. Girls in the community were often married by the time they were eighteen and never later than twenty. It had been several years since Thankful had started menstruating and her little-girl body had quickly taken on the shape of a young woman. Women were expected to be married when they came of age. Wives were expected to submit to their husbands—to be obedient in all ways and live in community with the others, owning nothing and sharing everything. That was God's plan. The only way to avoid this inevitability was through escape or death, and since she was not ready to kill herself, she had only one other choice. In a way, it was not unlike planning her death… but only in terms of the community she would leave behind. Her departure would be a beginning, not an ending, a leap into life. Then as soon as she could, she would start to look for her big sister.

Chapter Seventeen

❦

The crack and crash of a falling tree branch outside the house knocked out the lights, awakening Viridienne with an unpleasant shock and sending DT scrambling for cover. The cat didn't like sudden loud noises, and neither did Viridienne. It was three o'clock in the morning, and she'd fallen asleep in her chair. The house was dark—no power. She hauled herself up to her feet and, using her cell-phone flashlight to see in the sudden darkness, went to the door find out what had come down and where it had landed. The snow had pretty much stopped, but the weight of it must have been too much for the old tree that shaded the front of the house. A significant chunk of it lay directly in front of her car and across the path that led to her house. By some stroke of good fortune or divine intervention, it had missed her car completely.

I'll deal with it in the morning, she thought. *Nobody's going anywhere until the roads are clear, and out here in the boonies, it's anyone's guess when that'll happen. If worse comes to worst, and my phone dies, I can always go out and charge it in the car.*

She mentally congratulated herself on her lifelong habit of never letting the gas tank get less than a quarter full. She'd topped up earlier in the week and was good to go —when and if going anywhere was possible. Until then, she would be under house arrest.

For those first few precious moments after being startled awake, everything seemed normal. A broken branch, a snowy yard, a flashlight, and a sufficient wood supply. And then it all came rushing back—the gruesome image of her friend lying on the floor, the tragic waste of one so gifted, and the staggering weight of her own unspeakable shock and grief. She'd lost the one person in the world she'd trusted with her story.

A determined bubble of an idea pushed its way through her grief into her weary, tearful present. The police would do the criminal detective work and hopefully find the killer. That was their job.

But like the intricate tapestries and sculptures she created out of scraps, Viridienne found herself weaving together a totally different image. She would do the artistic investigation. She would find a way to tell the true story of Xenia Stamos and the incredible paintings that bore her indelible mark but not her name. Come hell or high water, she would bring the life and truth of the transcendent art of Rose-Xenia out of the shadows and into the light of day.

Then she remembered Rose warning her never to tell the story and mentioning the potential consequences to Viridienne's safety if she were ever to repeat the details they'd shared that one night. *But who would know?* Viridienne knew about witness-protection programs. *I should probably get in touch with Detective Fitzpatrick first thing in the morning.*

She was not by nature an impulsive woman, and now was not the time to be any different. Creating her fiber art, fixing up her falling-down house, and building a new life from the ground up took time and careful, deliberate thinking. Until the plan to uncover the truth about Rose's paintings was clear in her mind, she would speak of it to no one. If nothing else, Viridienne Greene knew how to keep secrets.

Yes. She nodded to herself. She would call Fitzpatrick. At the very least, she owed him a thank-you for his help and concern the night before. That, and she wanted to keep the door open for any future communication. The detective might be able to share new information that would help her in her personal mission.

With good reason, she was cautious and distrustful around men in power, and in her world, uniforms were power. But DI Fitzpatrick could have been her younger brother. She was older and taller than he was. He wore a uniform, but he didn't use it to threaten people or flaunt his authority. In the end, young as he was—or appeared to be—he'd made her feel safe and cared for when he answered the 911 call. He'd come through the door with compassionate authority and taken charge of everything.

She stepped back from the drafty door and made her way to the kitchen area, where she kept a flashlight, some matches, and a few candle stubs. After lighting and securing the candles, she pulled out the bedding she kept in the closet by the front door. The blankets were ice-cold, but a few moments of holding them up in front of the fire soon took care of that. She quickly smoothed it all onto the sofa where she and the cat would bed down for what was left of the night. After blowing out the candle and pulling the blanket tight around her shoulders, she closed her eyes and let DT purr her back to sleep.

Chapter Eighteen

W
hen the sun came up, brilliant orange at this time of year, it was blinding—and, after the dark fury of the day before, so very welcome. The power was still off, the house was chilly, and nothing was right with the world. But she and the cat were home and safe. She could throw a couple of logs on the woodstove, make herself a cup of coffee, cook them both some eggs, and then consider her next steps. DT was fond of scrambled eggs and was already circling her ankles in noisy, furry anticipation.

The coffee was surprisingly good, considering she used the old campfire trick of throwing a handful of coffee grounds into boiling water and hoping for the best. She did not drain the coffee through an old sock but through a regular coffee filter folded into a funnel fashioned out of aluminum foil. Thus fortified, she could move on to scrambling the eggs with far more confidence and clarity of mind.

After feeding herself and DT—with seconds for both —she located her cell phone and was more than grateful to find a few bars of power visible in the upper right-hand corner. With a second cup of coffee on the table beside her, she curled up in her chair, tapped in the number for the Plymouth Police headquarters, and asked for Detective Inspector Fitzpatrick.

I wonder if he has a first name. Note to self: ask him about that if I get the chance. Her musings were interrupted when he came on the line. She identified herself and thanked him for his help and concern the night before.

"How are you doing?" he asked. "You had a pretty rough day yesterday. You got any power out there?"

The concern in his voice was enough to shake what little control she'd been able to muster. She blinked back sudden tears and put on a brave voice.

"I'm not great, but I'm definitely better. This is going to take time. I lost power sometime last night while I was asleep. And if that wasn't enough, would you believe part of a tree came down all around my car last night? I seem to be batting a thousand. But it's morning. The sun's up, and I made it through the night."

"What about light? Can you see your way around?"

"I don't need candles to see to read or to knit as long as the sun is up, and I can cook what I want on the wood-stove, and I have loads of old candles. As far as food goes, I'm good, and anything that needs to be kept frozen is out on the porch." She stopped herself. *Why am I chattering on like this? What does he care about spoiled food?*

"Uh, you told me to call you if I remembered anything else. Well, I guess I have."

"Really? So soon?"

Viridienne rolled her eyes in frustration. "Really? *So soon* yourself, Detective. Think about it. I discovered my best friend dead, murdered in her own home. I was in total shock. When I think back on it, I'm surprised I was able to remember my own name. Now that I've had a few hours to calm down and get my head back on sort of straight, the first thing I did was to call you. Surely, I get some points for that."

"Of course. I'm sorry, Ms. Greene. I didn't mean to sound offhand. This has gotten to all of us. Grisly murders don't usually happen in beautiful historic Plymouth, America's folksy, friendly hometown. Do you want us to come out and talk to you there? We've got four-wheel drive, and the roads are still pretty bad."

Viridienne considered her answer. As a rule, she didn't like strangers inside her home unless she herself extended the invitation. And despite everything that had brought them together the night before, Alison and Fitzpatrick were still strangers—maybe less so than some, but strangers nonetheless. On the other hand, it was freezing out, and there was a fallen tree branch in a very inconvenient spot.

"I suppose that would make it easier for me. As I said, I had a branch come down, and while it didn't hit my car, it's blocked the drive, and I can't get the car out. So even though the house is nice and warm, it looks like I'm kind of stuck in it. So sure, come on out."

"Jaysus, Mary, and Joseph, woman, let's hope you get your power back before much longer. Um... let me see what I can do from here. I might be able to make a few phone calls. How about we come by in about an hour, around ten? I'll be bringing Alison with me, and as long as we're there, I'll have a look and see what I can do about getting the branch off your car."

"Wow. Thank you. Uh… do you need directions?"

"Nope. Just the street address, miss. This is my beat, remember? And besides, we have GPS in all of our vehicles. Government issue."

Viridienne, despite living in the modern world for all this time, was still getting used to the advances in technology. "I live on Skye Pond Lane. There are only two houses on the street—mine is the second one. It's right on the pond. I guess I'll see you in a little while. And Detective?"

"Yes, miss?"

"One more time, thank you."

Fitzpatrick mumbled a response.

Chapter Nineteen

While Viridienne was trying to pull herself together and organize her thoughts, in downtown Plymouth and beyond, the grisly news was all anyone was talking about. The name of the victim might have been withheld until notification of the next of kin, but news traveled fast in a small town. Within less than twenty-four hours, everyone in Plymouth knew that Rose Doré, a reclusive artist living in a quiet family neighborhood, had been viciously murdered in her own home.

At the Mayflower Gallery, the volunteers were beyond stunned. Despite the news reports and the town-wide shock about what had happened the day before, they'd dutifully trudged in to hang the show, not out of disrespect or indifference to what had happened but out of a profound sense of loss and outrage and a need to be with people who knew and loved her. And now that they were all there, no one knew what to do or say. Several were given to fits of weeping, while others had cups of untouched coffee in front of them. They were collectively in shock.

They hadn't been there for more than twenty minutes when the telephone jangled them into a numb reality. Bob DeLaar reached for the handset and mechanically recited the scripted greeting taped to the top of the desk in front of the phone. It was the Plymouth police, saying they would be there in five minutes and not to let anybody move or touch Ms. Doré's paintings.

"Evidence," the caller said. "Possible forensic evidence."

After Bob had hung up the phone, he directed Jackson to double-check the location of the paintings so there would be no delay in showing them to the police. By eleven in the morning, the police had come and gone, taking all three of Rose's paintings with them, explaining that there might be fingerprints or DNA that would lead them to something… or someone.

"Fingerprints, all right," huffed Pauline. "How many would you like? I'm sure mine will be all over them—I moved them. And Jackson's too. He brought them here. Anyone else here touch or handle them?" Two hands went up.

"Wonderful! Just wonderful. I wonder how many of us will be brought in for questioning."

"Calm down, dear," said Karen Connors, another one of the regular volunteers. "Nobody is accusing anybody. We were all here most of the day yesterday, and if we weren't right here, we damn sure weren't anywhere near Rose's house. Besides…" Her voice cracked. "We all knew she was a little strange, but dammit, we loved her."

"I was at her house yesterday," said a somber-faced Jackson Smith. "Remember me telling you I went there the night before to bring back one of the paintings? She wanted to fix something. She called me early yesterday morning, and I went back to pick it up. She was fine then —even gave me a cup of coffee. I can't believe this. She was fine. She even gave me a cup of coffee." He lifted a fist to his open mouth. "Oh my God, I was probably the last person to see her alive. The last person. Oh my God."

Jackson had a habit of repeating himself when he was stressed or anxious. At the moment, he was both. They all were.

"What do we do now?" asked Vaughn.

Karen spoke up. "Rose would never want us to cancel. I say we go ahead and hang the show... and we'll hang it in her honor but cancel the opening reception. I don't know about you, but while I don't mind keeping busy and hanging paintings, I damn sure couldn't go to a happy, laughy, chatty party."

The gallery director, Pauline DeLaar, took charge. She was all business, and everyone was relieved to have her do it. "That works. Besides, it would be a total pain to have everybody come back and get their work. Then what would we do? I mean, we can't close our doors just because someone died... I mean..." She flushed and invented a coughing fit to cover her embarrassment. "I guess I didn't say that very well." Pauline faltered a second time, looking for a way to extricate herself. Finding none, she changed direction. "Okay, everybody, I guess it's all hands on deck. I'll call the local radio and TV stations and announce the cancellation of the reception. After that, I'll send out a mass email to all the members. That should do it."

She stopped for breath and pointed to the phone on the desk. "And I've already put a message on the answering machine and switched it to automatic. That way, it won't be ringing off the hook while we're mounting the show. That would push me over the edge, and I have to tell you, I'm damn close to it now. Oh, and before I forget it, thank you, Jackson, for clearing and sanding the walk and steps. What would we ever do without you?"

He ducked his head, smiled, and pointed to the other man in the room. "It wasn't just me. Vaughn came in early too. He helped."

The director stood. Quietly, without her usual authoritative enthusiasm, she said, "Well, then, I guess it's decided. Let's get on with it."

Chapter Twenty

Viridienne rubbed her eyes and tried to focus her thoughts. *I need a washup. I'll begin by making another pan of coffee,* she told herself, *and while it's stewing, I'll have a shower and get dressed. On second thought, I have no power and therefore no hot water, so I guess I won't. Damn! On to plan B. At least I have cold water!*

She filled a spaghetti pot, set it on the woodstove, hoping she had time for a quick sponge bath before the police detectives arrived. After collecting the necessary accoutrements for the bathing ritual, she spread out a towel on the rug in front of the stove and dropped her nightgown onto the floor beside her. She hummed and purred in sensual pleasure as the soap and hot water worked their healing magic, blotting out for a few moments the shock and heartbreak of the last twenty-four hours. Everything looked and felt better after a good wash and a fresh cup of coffee. She looked at the clock, counted the remaining minutes, and quickly pulled on cold jeans, a fresh shirt, and an oversized sweater.

Detective Fitzpatrick was apologetic when he arrived a half hour later than expected. He and Detective Grey stamped their feet and brushed the windblown snow off their arms and shoulders before entering the house. He was carrying a box of doughnuts. She could smell them the moment he opened the door.

"The roads are still pretty bad. Yours isn't the only place with a branch or even a whole tree down. You got lucky, though—I think we can move it off to one side and get you out."

She tried to smile, but it still took too much effort. "That would be great, but we can talk about that later. I've got some fresh coffee." She held up the saucepan.

"Oh yeah." Fitzpatrick was smiling and nodding enthusiastically.

She realized, standing there with pot in hand, that she was actually seeing what the detectives looked like for the first time. He was of medium height, solid and muscular, pale but pink cheeked from the cold. She could not make out the color of his eyes from across the room, but there was no mistaking the color and texture of his hair: red curls. Detective Grey stood almost as tall as Detective Fitpatrick and was just beginning to thicken around the middle. Her straight hair fell only to her chin—practical, no-nonsense hair.

"You can hang your coats on the back of the door. There's a peg rack there."

Viridienne cleared a place at the table and set out three flowered china mugs. "I knew someone one who used to call my coffee 'battery acid.' She said it was so strong it you could stand a spoon in it. I've improved. The stuff I make now's a little better than that. How do you take it?"

"Black, no sugar," said Fitzpatrick. "You Swedish or German or something? You kinda look it. Ever since I did that Ancestry thing, I'm interested in where people come from. I'm three-hundred-percent Irish, in case you're wondering. I was hoping for something more interesting. Nada. The only way I could be more Irish is if I was a boiled potato." He smiled and touched his finger to the side of his nose.

Viridienne understood that his light chatter was intended to soften the gravity of the situation. He took the chair by the window as she worked her way through the multiple steps of making the coffee. She felt him watching her.

"Half Swedish. The other side is English and Irish... I think. I guess I don't really know. It wasn't anything we talked about when I was little. In my family, you just were part of the family. People didn't care about nationality or ancestry."

He looked curious but said nothing.

"I'll have the same, plain black," said Alison. "And for the record, would you believe English and Polish? Now, there's a combination for you. Father's English, mother's Polish. Let's just say that ours was not a calm and peaceful household. Lotsa fun, though." She smiled.

"Well, that's easy, then. Black coffee times three." Viridienne filled the three cups and moved toward the investigative team. "Here you go." She set the cups on the table, and Fitzpatrick lifted the cover of the cardboard bakery box and held it out to the two women. She hadn't paid it much attention when he'd first come in, but now she was all eyes and couldn't decide between a honey-dipped confection and a cinnamon-dusted cruller. Given that she could eat like a horse and never gain a pound, she settled on the biggest and the most familiar—the cruller.

Using the pastry as a pointer, she directed their attention to the tapestries, weavings, and quilts that covered the walls. "In case you're interested, this is my day job. I'm a fiber artist. And if you haven't ever heard of that, I make art with yarn and thread and fabric. I met Rose at the Mayflower Gallery. We both taught classes and exhibited our work there."

The two police detectives dutifully looked to where she was pointing.

"It takes up a lot of room in a small house. But it's just me and the cat and the spider plant in here. My actual studio is over there." She pointed to a closed door. "But it's like an igloo right now. It's a good thing yarn doesn't freeze. Now, if I were a painter, I'd worry…" And then she crumpled into tears. The word *painter* had brought it all back: her friend, the murder, and the reason why two police detectives were sitting at her kitchen table.

Fitzpatrick busied himself picking out a jelly doughnut. Then he took a long sip of his coffee, leaned against the back of his chair, and slowly bit into the decadent, dense raspberry pastry, giving Viridienne a few minutes to collect herself. For a man trained in dealing with unpleasantness— a man who carried a gun—he was surprisingly kind and easy to talk to. Funny even.

"I know about yarn and fabric. My granny made Irish

fisherman sweaters, and my mother made quilts out of the clothes we grew out of. They were sturdy, and we were warm, but they were really pretty too. My mother and grandmother didn't think of themselves as artists. It's just what they did at the end of the day when the housework was done. We didn't have much money, and if we wanted something, we had to make it." He smiled. Then, as if turning a switch, he set down his cup, took out his note pad and pencil, and became all business. Alison pulled a small digital recorder out of her handbag.

"Do you mind if we tape the conversation? It really helps to have the actual words of a witness and not just the written notes. Is that okay?"

"Witness?" said Viridienne, suddenly alarmed. "When did I become a witness? Hold on. Maybe you should wait a minute before we start taping. I need to make sure of something first. It's about this witness-protection thing. You are not going to use my name on anything that goes public, are you?"

"Is that a problem?" asked Fitzpatrick.

She hesitated, remembering a fierce-eyed Rose Doré warning her never to repeat what she'd said that night. She could still feel Rose grabbing her arm and saying, "They told me if anything ever got out about this, they would go after my family and anyone else who might know and could interrupt their operation." Viridienne had promised, but Rose was dead. *Does that make the promise null and void?* She rubbed her chin, pondering the possible consequences, not sure how much she would say.

Fitzpatrick tapped his pencil on the notepad. "I don't understand. The woman is dead. She can't hurt you, but it's possible that what you know and what you are able to say could help us find who killed her."

Viridienne looked at the man sitting across from her. "My best friend would never hurt me... but she did warn me about something. I think she knew she was being watched. When she told me her story, she made me promise I'd never repeat any of it. Not one word. She was protecting me, and she wasn't kidding. I need to know my name will never be mentioned and that you'll make no reference to me other than I was the one who found her. Once I have your word on that, I'll tell you why I need that assurance and everything I know."

"I don't see that as a problem," said Fitzpatrick. "How bad can it be? In this business, there isn't much we haven't seen or heard. Why don't we just get started? You can stop anytime. We can't force you to talk if you don't want to."

"I want to... and I have to," she said, becoming steady in her resolve. "She was my friend. It's the least I can do. She's dead, and she doesn't have children anybody can threaten or hurt so what difference would it make now if everything comes out?"

Viridienne took a sip of coffee, more for courage than from thirst, and began to tell the convoluted and tragic story of how Xenia Stamos became Rose Doré. She told them, in detail, a long, complicated, and terribly unhappy story of a woman whose one passion in life was painting— a tale of abuse, plagiarism, false accusation, life threats, and eventually, a payoff in return for silence. Rose's distant past was certainly not of importance anymore, but Viridienne still included details that went far back.

Telling the tale was far more difficult than she'd

thought it would be, because it brought up so many painful memories that were buried deep in her own past. But she had to tell it because Rose was a friend. They'd spoken the same language. Speaking the truth was not a choice—it was her duty. She would do all she could to help bring the murderer to justice.

My gran sat in her chair and knitted
She didn't talk much
She smiled even less
She was too busy catching hold of the memories
And knitting them into the hats
And the sweaters and the mittens
Before she lost them forever.

Chapter Twenty-One

❧❀❧

O bedient Thankful's opportunity for deliverance came when she least expected it on a day when the entire community was involved in preparations for a family wedding. As luck would have it, and because she lived up to every letter of the word *obedient*, Thankful could be sent outside on business errands or collection or delivery runs with one of the brothers. That day, they were off to collect food and drink for the celebration. She lived for these trips. She loved being outside the walls and seeing the houses and the people and the cars, seeing the other world... but just as much, she relished the simple smell of the fresh, free air.

Few members of the community were allowed beyond the clearly marked boundaries surrounding the compound, and she was positively giddy with anticipation. A trip outside was a rare pleasure, a little teaser taste of the forbidden fruit of freedom. On previous errand runs, when she was sure no one was looking, she'd picked up local

tourist brochures, newspapers, and even real estate magazines—anything she could hide in her deep apron pockets,
drop into her pouch, or stuff inside her blouse until she got
home. She was good, grabbing just enough but not so
much that anyone would notice any unexplainable lumps
or bulges in her clothing.

That day, she sat, belted in next to Elder Thomas,
silently looking out of the window. To the casual observer,
she was the very picture of the quiet, docile, submissive
woman so highly valued in the community. What the
casual observer could not see was her fists clenched
together under her apron and her shaking knees well
hidden under her long skirt. The map and list of phone
numbers and addresses that she now carried with her
everywhere was rolled into a tight tube and curled into her
bra under her left breast.

In her apparent composure, she was noting every sign
and street name. For the last year, she'd been actively planning the escape that would happen, right out of the blue,
on one of these routine trips and at one of the scheduled
stops. *Today could be the day*, she thought. Where and when
were still in question. It all depended on whether they
stopped for gas at the place she'd chosen to make her
getaway.

She knew they would stop for gas somewhere. They
always did, and when they did, Elder Thomas would get
out of the van, hook up the nozzle, and go off to use the
men's room. The routine never varied.

Her opportunity came when he pulled into a combination filling station and convenience store. She was almost
afraid to breathe. This was the one. She'd picked it as the

best possibility because of its location on the highway and the way the little convenience store itself was laid out.

When they stopped and the gas pump was running, she remained in the van until she saw him enter the restroom and pull the door shut behind him. In one swift movement, she slipped down off the high seat of the van and raced toward a car that was just leaving the station. She ran around the front of the car to the driver's side and banged on the window then watched in fear and desperation as the driver deliberately turned away and drove off.

Chapter Twenty-Two

"I don't get it." Fitzpatrick was swirling his coffee. "You say they threatened her life if she ever even showed one of her paintings. Why didn't she just stop altogether? Why in the world did she take the chance and start painting again?"

Viridienne bit her lip. She wasn't losing her resolve, but she was physically and emotionally exhausted. This was so damned hard. She took a steadying breath. "First of all, her real name is Xenia Stamos. Rose Doré is the name she took after her husband died. That was another part of the deal. No one would think of asking a woman named Rose Doré about the paintings of a man named Nicolo Brandosi."

She blew her nose, wiped her eyes, and continued. "It was some time after she came here before she painted anything for herself. But an artist makes art. It's what we do. We don't really have a choice. What she was painting in her husband's name wasn't hers anymore."

She paused to calm herself and collect her thoughts before going on. "I'm an artist. Making art is like breathing. We have to do it because if we don't, we die inside. The whole time she was turning out the so-called *forgotten masterpieces* for the Brandosi family, she was quietly working on her own again. She was really careful. She would never allow photographs to be taken of herself or her work. I have no idea how they found out."

"That's what we'd like to know," said Fitzpatrick. "There's a hell of a lot going on here, and I suspect we've only scratched the surface. What you've said so far suggests organized crime. They have tentacles everywhere. Everyone knows there's a huge presence in the Providence area. And it's also well known that one of the more lucrative ventures for organized crime is dealing in stolen or expertly forged art." He bit his lip. "She should have moved farther away—done something else with her time."

Viridienne threw up her hands. "She had nothing but what they chose to give her. She'd been through a living nightmare. She never had children, and she felt she needed to stay near her family. Remember, Detective, they not only threatened her, but they also threatened to hurt her family if she said anything. Even though she had almost no contact with her family, they were all she had. They were told that if anyone asked about her, they should say that she'd had a complete nervous breakdown after the death of her husband and was in a place where she was safe and could be cared for. Their silence was another part of the deal."

"Jesus, they covered all the bases, didn't they?" Fitzpatrick shook his head as Alison attended to the recorder.

"From what she told me, her life depended on it. I'd be careful too. Wouldn't you? That's why I made you promise to keep my name out of it. I mean, as far as I know, they have no idea that I exist. But Rose was adamant. She was trying to protect me."

The idea that had started taking shape in Viridienne's mind the night before was beginning to crystalize. She'd learned a long time ago that it was easier and quicker to ask for forgiveness than for permission. Even better than that was not getting found out at all. She would ask parallel questions and learn as much as she could from the professionals in this game without revealing her own hand—at least, not yet.

Viridienne cocked her head, looking directly at the detective sitting across the table from her, and then, very deliberately, pivoted. "I have a question, and it's on an entirely different subject."

He leaned back in the chair and crossed his arms over his chest. "And that is…?"

"Maybe I shouldn't ask this, but do you have a first name? It only says Fitzpatrick on your ID badge."

He covered his eyes with his hand and started to laugh. Alison rolled her eyes and looked at the ceiling. Viridienne's question had broken the tension.

"Where did that come from? I suppose it's a fair question. Since we seem to be telling secrets, I might as well tell you mine."

"Is there something…?" Viridienne raised a curious eyebrow and glanced over at Alison, who was smiling fondly at her partner.

"Oh, she knows. There's not much about me she

doesn't. I do have a first name, and it's Patrick. Irish as Paddy's pig, it is—and dyed-in-the-wool Irish Catholic with it. Patrick Fitzpatrick. Remember what I said about being one step removed from a boiled potato? Curly red hair and all." He shook his head, grinning broadly. "No way in hell was I going through life as Pat, or Paddy Fitzpaddy. 'Patrick Fitzpatrick' comes out sounding like someone with a really bad stutter. In my midteens, I discarded my first name altogether and became Fitzpatrick. At least it wasn't Paddy or Fitzy… I will answer to Fitz with my friends but never while in uniform." He stopped, stood up, and rubbed the back of his neck. "And changing the subject for a second time, I don't know about you, but I've been sitting way too long. I need a seventh-inning stretch."

Chapter Twenty-Three

After an unsettled night of lying in bed and getting nowhere near sleep, the man got up and made himself a cup of coffee. The ritual of opening the container, grinding the beans, and boiling the water was the most normal thing he'd done in twenty-four hours. The sound of the grinder, the smell of the freshly ground beans and the feel of the hot coffee against his cold hands made everything seem a little better.

Then the early-morning TV news anchor spoke the words he'd been waiting to hear. "Yesterday evening, a local artist was found brutally murdered in her home in Plymouth. An investigation is underway, and as of now, details are sketchy. But from the nature of the crime and the condition of the body, it would appear this was not a random act and was likely committed by someone who was known to the victim. The name is being withheld pending notification of the next of kin. Anyone having any…"

He clicked off the mournful-looking reporter mid-sentence and tried to concentrate on his coffee. He was surprised to find that hearing the truth of what he'd done reported on public media had totally unsettled him. Hearing someone else speak the words describing what he had so recently done removed any sense of nightmarish unreality. It wasn't a bad dream anymore. It was real. He'd killed her. It was finally over.

He swallowed the last of his coffee, hoping it would wash away the troubling thoughts. It didn't. He was restless, but it was too early to go anywhere. Nothing but coffee shops and twenty-four-hour convenience stores were open. He got up from the table and jogged in place for a few minutes to release some of the tension that was making it hard for him to breathe.

By the time he'd run long enough to crack a sweat, he could feel his mind clearing and his thoughts beginning to coalesce. *It wouldn't hurt to do a quick check on that oversized, weird, butchy-looking friend of hers. Who knows what she might know.*

"If you are going to do something," his grandfather always told him, "then do it right, or don't do it all." He'd have to think about that. And because there was no way in hell anyone would know who he was or would connect him to Rose, he couldn't see any harm in going back to Plymouth and hanging out in one of the local coffee shops.

Greasy spoons were where the townies went for breakfast and local gossip. Neighborhood bars, the ones off the tourist route—the places without trendy names or exotic drink menus, where the townies went for a beer after work.

That was where a man who was willing to listen could learn the real local news without ever turning on the TV.

He looked at his watch. It would be daylight within the hour. He could be there in time to catch the breakfast crowd.

Chapter Twenty-Four

After two detectives, one artist, and a one-eyed cat had a chance to get up and stretch, Viridienne resettled herself at the wooden table with another doughnut—coconut this time—and continued with Rose's story.

"Rose…" She paused. "She was Rose when I met her, so I guess I'll always think of her as Rose. Anyway, after a few months in her new place here in Plymouth, she started walking around town, getting to know people very slowly and very carefully. That's when she found the Mayflower Gallery. She must have been drawn to it, sorta like a bee to honey.

"At first, she volunteered at the Mayflower as a gallery sitter. You know, sitting there, smiling and answering questions, telling people how to find the bathroom and where to get a drink of water. I suppose it was so she could be near something familiar. She could be out and involved with people but not too close and personal, if you know what I mean."

Fitzpatrick and Alison both nodded, but from the look in their eyes, it was

not clear that they fully understood. Viridienne continued with her story.

"Pretty soon, she volunteered to do some teaching. At first, it was only in the children's classes. Art was all she knew, so it stands to reason that's where she'd go, right? She was lonely. That's understandable. She needed some kind of a social life, and this fit the bill. She was a great teacher, and the kids loved her. Couldn't get enough of her, really. She never had kids of her own, so maybe that was part of it. Anyway, she loved it."

Alison nodded sympathetically.

"Well, you can imagine what happened. It wasn't long before they talked her into teaching some adult classes. That's when people started asking about her own art and what it was like. No one knew she'd been painting at home for years—paintings that were to be passed off as undiscovered Brandosis… and other paintings of her own, signed with her new name, which she'd locked away in the attic of that monster of a house."

Viridienne shook her head. "I was her best friend, and it was years before I even knew they were there. I think somebody came a couple of times a year and collected the newly discovered 'Brandosis.'" She made air quotations around the name. "Eventually, I must have passed some kind of test. Who knows? Anyway, she finally let me see them. We were a funny pair, you know. I'm six feet tall, and she was just over five feet. I felt like a gawky great blue heron next to a feisty little chickadee."

Fitzgerald eased her back into focus. "What are her paintings like?"

The memory was enough to bring on a new gush of tears. When she was able to continue, she said, "Breathtaking. Like nothing I've ever seen." More tears. "I can't believe she'll never paint again."

It was time for another break. Viridienne needed a rest. This time, Fitzpatrick suggested he make them some tea if she had any, saying that he, for one, was coffeed out.

"Tea is the all-purpose Irish cure for whatever it is that ails ye, or so my sainted mother would say." He smiled.

Viridienne pointed toward a cabinet over the sink, and Alison refilled the kettle and set it back on the woodstove.

When they started up again, Fitzpatrick asked, "So how come you went to her house last night? Were you just dropping in for a visit?"

Viridienne shook her head. "As close as we were, I never went there without calling. Nobody *dropped in* on Rose. Last night was a first. I went there because I was worried about her. I was afraid if I called her and asked about the missing painting, she'd totally freak out."

"Why so?"

"You'd have to have known her. We're having a members show at the Mayflower, and she'd entered three paintings under the name of Rose Doré. She'd been showing her work regularly for a while. It's totally different from anything she painted under Nicolo's name. Different, but every bit as brilliant. God knows how she managed that—she was so gifted. Your art bears your signature whether you want it to or not. But the woman really did paint in two different styles. Anyway, she only exhibited her work at the Mayflower, and it was never photographed or offered for public sale. She told me that she did sell them occasionally out of her house, but it was always very hush-hush.

"Everybody thought it was one more of her quirks, and we just went along with her. As I understand it, she'd dropped the paintings off at the gallery the day before, three of them, and the next day, when it was time for the judging, one of them wasn't there. Gone!"

"What happened?"

"Well, that's what I went to find out. It was supposed to have been returned earlier that day. But it wasn't... well, not while I was there."

"And that's when you found her."

Viridienne nodded.

"You said you knew where she kept her own paintings?"

She gave another nod and a tearful gulp. "Like I said, she only took me up there once. I never told anyone about them. I mean, people asked because they knew I was her friend. I just played along with the quirky-artist theory and said I didn't know. What I did know was that she was taking her life in her hands every time she picked up a brush... but she couldn't not do it. I got that. The creative spirit doesn't take no for an answer. Ask me—I know. Look at this place. It's what I do all the time. I'd probably have done the same thing Rose did. All I know is somebody somewhere must have found out she was painting again... and they killed her for it."

"Why?"

"I told you."

"Tell me again, please."

Viridienne closed her eyes, took in a long breath, and slowly let it out. "Rose told me that the Brandosi family had claimed the rights to all of the paintings done under her husband's name. They're worth millions now. If the truth ever got out, the game would be over. No more lost paintings to discover. Of course, the existing ones would still be of enormous value, but the shame of it all would follow the family name forever and possibly land several of them in jail. Art theft and art fraud are not something you hear a lot about in Plymouth, but like you just said, it's big business—big, dirty, dangerous business. Don't think for a minute the only thing the Mafia controls are restaurants and waste disposal."

He nodded. "You're not telling me anything I don't know, miss, and as you think about all of this, I'm sure there will be more you can tell us in the next few days and weeks. Given a little time, things you know and remember about Rose and how she lived will bubble up to the surface. That's normal under these circumstances. You're still pretty shaken up. But you've already given us a lot to work with… and I understand why you wouldn't want your name used in connection with any of this. I'll do my best."

Viridienne went wide-eyed. "What?"

He shifted uncomfortably on the wooden chair. "I don't see any reason to mention your name, and like I said, I'll do my best to see that it doesn't happen."

Viridienne caught hold of his arm. "What are you

talking about? You said… what about witness protection? I may be an artist, but even I know about that."

He waved her down. "Easy there. I have every intention of keeping your name out of it. But everyone knows you were her best friend. Your best friend was brutally murdered. It's already in the papers and on the news. I'm surprised reporters haven't been beating down your door, but I think the storm helped you out on that score."

He continued. "There'll be an investigation. It's obligatory. If we get lucky and we find the killer, there'll be a trial. One way or another, your name is already connected to this. You found her. I'll do everything in my power to leave it at that. But if anyone approaches you about this, I'd say nothing if I were you… and I mean *nothing*. Not to reporters, not to somebody who says they're representing the family, and if a TV truck shows up outside, don't answer the door. You know what your mother told you— don't talk to strangers."

Viridienne turned to ice inside. Her mother had told her nothing. There were no strangers in the Obedient Believers. They were all one big loving family community. *Sure they were.*

Chapter Twenty-Five

"Hey, are you all right?" Fitzpatrick's question pulled her out of the chilling flashback and back into the room.

Viridienne shook her head. "No. I'm done. Shot. I feel like I'm going to pass out. Enough is enough! *Fini!*"

Alison ran and got her a glass of water as Fitzpatrick put away his notepad and pencil. "I'm sorry," he said. "We have gone on too long. In these situations, the first responses are often the most helpful." He shrugged apologetically. "I'm doing my job, but I have to tell you, there are some days that it's a lot harder than others."

She smiled weakly. "I understand. I've had an awful shock, and I still can't really believe it——" She stopped mid-sentence. "Oh Jesus... we've got to tell her family."

Fitzpatrick nodded and said softly, "That was going to be my next question. I was hoping that someone would come forward when it hit the news. Do you have any idea how to get in touch with them?"

"It's already on the news? I don't watch much TV, and besides"—she pointed to a lamp on the table—"there's no power."

"It's on the news, all right, but unless it's exceptionally grisly or the people are high-profile, local Boston news— much less Plymouth docsn't usually play in Providence. How long it will continue to be newsworthy, and how far up the interest scale it goes, depends on who gets involved. And for your safety and that of the rest of her family, let's hope it stays on the back pages."

Viridienne went into her studio and dug around in her filing cabinet. A few minutes later, she was back, holding a sheet of paper.

"I found it. She gave this to me a few months ago. I made a copy just in case I misplaced the original. She said that if I ever needed to contact her family, this was how I could do it. I wonder if she had some kind of a premonition." She shook her head. "What a waste."

Fitzpatrick looked at it then folded it into quarters and slipped it into his inside pocket. "I said it once, and I'll say it again: I think we've only just begun to scratch the surface of this whole thing, and even this much is ugly as hell. I don't want to scare you, Viridienne, but it appears that we are dealing with some very nasty and vindictive individuals who will stop at nothing to get what they want or to protect their interests. If you come across anything at all that seems even the slightest bit suspicious, I want you let me know. If you feel you are being watched, or you get strange phone calls, or someone you don't know shows up at the door, I want you to call me at once. Is that understood? And remember to lock your doors."

She nodded. "So when are you going to tell her family?"

"Do they know of you and your friendship with Rose?"

"I doubt it. She had almost no contact with them. She sent them cards at Christmas and Easter. It broke her heart to be like that, but she had no choice. She was trying to protect them. I don't think they even knew her other name."

Fitzpatrick stood and reached for his jacket. Alison did the same.

"We'd better get going, but before we do, we'll get that branch out of the way for you so you can get out. Does this street actually get plowed, or do you have to ride the ruts until it melts?"

Viridienne actually laughed. "A little of each. If it's a really big storm, they plow. I never know. Usually, I cross my fingers and ride the ruts. This one was hard-hitting while it was coming down, but it didn't last long. Technically, this is a private road. Just my luck."

"I'll make a few calls and see what I can do," he said then added in a husky voice, "I got connections."

Viridienne touched his forearm with the tips of her fingers. "Thank you, Fitz... for everything. I mean it. You've been very kind."

He paused and then put his hand over his heart. "Just doin' my job, ma'am. It's pretty isolated out here. You sure you'll be all right?"

"How about this: I'll call you if I think I'm not."

"Deal," said Detective Inspector Fitzpatrick.

In less than ten minutes, Fitzpatrick tapped on her front door to tell her they'd moved the branch and cleared off her car. She was good to go if she wanted to. Viridienne thanked him and waved them off.

When they were gone, she added a log to the woodstove and collapsed into her favorite chair. She was too exhausted to even think about picking up her knitting needles, which were often a source of relaxation as well as one of her creative outlets. The basket overflowing with brightly colored and richly textured yarns, always within arm's reach, remained untouched. Even DT knew better than to disturb her and curled up on the floor next to her feet.

Fitzpatrick was right, she mused—there was more to this. She'd let him do the detecting and investigating. That was his job. Somewhere in Rhode Island, a family was about to learn that their beautiful, talented, tortured daughter had been viciously murdered by someone who knew exactly what he was doing. Right there and then, she vowed to sit down with them and tell them about the good years their daughter had enjoyed in her new life in Plymouth. She would tell them about the big beautiful house that their daughter had lived in, about the children whose lives she'd enriched with her teaching, and—one day—about the paintings that were still there, locked away until it was safe to bring them out.

Suddenly, she felt better. She had a job to do, and—by the god she refused to name and wanted nothing to do with—come hell or high water, she'd do it. The police would take care of solving the crime of the murder and telling the family about it. She would see that the crime of the decade-long forgery would be uncovered as well. She couldn't give Rose back her life, but she could give her back her name and her art.

Viridienne looked up at the clock on the wall. *Is it only twelve-thirty in the afternoon?* She felt as though she'd been up for a week.

Chapter Twenty-Six

B ack in the comforting warmth of the police car,
the two detectives were comparing notes. The
roads were clear, and the driving was easier, and
with any luck at all, they'd be back to HQ before one
o'clock. They could stop off at a drive-through for a quick
bite to eat and still make it back in plenty of time. The
wind had dropped, so they weren't being buffeted by
blowing snow, and it was a spectacularly beautiful day—
bright sun, electric-blue sky, and fresh snow still blanketing
the trees. In twenty-four hours, it would all be flattened
down by cars and begrimed by sand trucks, but at the
moment, it was lovely. Their conversation was anything
but.

"So what do you think?" asked Fitzpatrick as he drove.

"I think we need to ask more questions."

"Why do you say that?"

Grey made a face. "I'm not sure. A woman is dead,
and her best friend finds her. The best friend has the key to

the house and says she never dropped in without calling first. But this time, she did. I want to know what Viridienne Greene was doing five to six hours earlier that day."

Fitzpatrick shook his head. "Standard line of reasoning, but I don't think for one minute she had anything to do with it. Rose Doré was killed by a man—a strong man who knew exactly what he was doing. A professional. Besides, you saw how broken up Viridienne was. You can't fake that."

"So how did he get into the house? There was no sign of a struggle or forced entry. I don't think she's told us everything. People are weird. Professional jealousy gone crazy? Wouldn't be the first time that's happened. So maybe she didn't actually do it herself, but she could have arranged it."

Fitzpatrick felt doubtful, but Alison was on a roll. "Maybe it was someone she knew. Maybe the guy had a key. You're convinced she was killed by a man?"

Fitzpatrick nodded. "Women don't usually take someone out with a single blow to the back of the head. Women don't usually kill. This was a hit job if I ever saw one."

Fitzpatrick signaled for a left turn and skidded slightly as he rounded the corner. "Whoops! Now, where were we? Oh yeah. You think Viridienne might have had something to do with it. I don't agree. If the story of the husband's family and the conditions of her life in Plymouth are true, then I can see the Brandosi family hiring a professional to do it. She broke the rules, and she paid. Plain and simple. No second chances. Let's just hope they don't go after the family as well. Remember, when she left her husband, she ran to her brother. Then all of a sudden, Brandosi has a tragic accident. You do the math."

Alison shook her head. "I thought I'd heard it all, but that whole thing is pretty hard to believe. Why didn't her family do more to protect her? Where the hell were they when all this was going on? I could never *not* have contact with one of my children. I don't care what I was threatened with. It's not making sense."

"Alison, I don't want to play the age-and-experience card or to sound patronizing, but you simply haven't seen as many domestic violence cases as I have. I grew up in South Boston, remember? There's an Irish mafia, too, you know. Nobody ever talked about it, but somehow, everybody knew. And the one thing everybody knew was that you didn't cross them. You played along, and you shut up, and they protected you... for money. When you get warring families with connections going at each other—a Rhode Island Mafia Italian family versus a tight-knit Greek family—then it's an eye for an eye, and that's only the beginning. The bad greasy dago husband hurt their precious virgin Greek daughter. She kept it quiet. Abused women often do until the day they don't. She told her brother... and the brother made a few phone calls, and all of a sudden, the guy takes a fall in the bathtub, and it's bye-bye for him."

He slowed and signaled for a right turn. "You can bet your bottom dollar the husband's family knows what happened, only they don't want any kind of investigation. So they shut up for the time being. And I'll bet you anything the supposed bathtub incident she told us about was no accident. I should probably look into that."

"That's ancient history. It's not going to help this case."

"Don't be so sure."

Alison threw up her hands. It was a familiar gesture. "So why did she go into hiding and basically disown her parents?"

"I told you. She was protecting them, and they were protecting her. They knew the rules. It was part of the deal. As long as she stayed out of the picture and no one broke silence, then it was a negotiated truce. Complicit silence for the health and safety of all concerned."

"And then she started painting again."

He nodded. "And somehow, someone in Rhode Island got wind of it. Maybe a tourist, for God's sake, took a cell phone shot and posted it on Facebook. Who the hell knows? There's no such thing as privacy anymore. They were probably trolling her. Doesn't take any brains these days. Any idiot with a cell phone can stalk someone."

Alison shuddered. "I suppose we don't see a lot of mob activity here in Plymouth."

"Don't kid yourself. It's another variant of *don't ask, don't tell* right here in our own backyard."

"I still think we need to talk to Viridienne again."

"I agree with you, but not because I think she's hiding anything. She's still not thinking straight, poor kid." He shook his head. "Jaysus, Mary, and Joseph, will you listen to me? She's hardly a kid. She's older than I am. Now, where was I?"

"Don't ask, don't tell?"

"Close enough. I'll call her in a few days, or she'll call us. It'll happen. I don't mind telling you, I can't help feeling sorry for her. Shit luck, really. I get the feeling she's totally on her own as well. Not one word about her own family. You notice that? No wonder they made a good pair."

"It's not our job to feel sorry for them, Fitz. We need to find out who killed her friend, not throw a pity party for her."

"I know. Page four, paragraph three: you don't have any friends when you're on a job. I hear you."

She gave him a sympathetic look. "It's usually my first reaction as well, but we both know it can muddy the waters."

"I hear you," said Fitz. "I promise never to feel sorry for anyone older than myself... or bigger than my head."

Alison responded with a giggle and a soft smack on his shoulder.

Fitzpatrick cleared his throat. He was all business once again. "I hate telling a family their kid is dead. I fucking hate it." Fitzpatrick didn't often swear.

She nodded. "You want me to make the call?"

"Nah, I'll do it. The sooner the better. Best case scenario is we get hold of them and go right down there and get it over with today."

"Gonna be a long day, then, my friend."

"That's why we get the big bucks, lady."

Chapter Twenty-Seven

Minutes after Obedient Thankful leapt out of the pickup, Elder Thomas came out to the van and discovered she wasn't sitting in the passenger seat. At first, he assumed she'd gone off to the ladies' room. But when the minutes passed, and she didn't return, he became concerned. He went around to the side of the building and found the door standing open and the bathroom empty. Panicked and angry, he thought how he would be held responsible and therefore disciplined for her disappearance. That, and that he'd been considering taking her as a second wife for himself. *Calm down. Think.*

He ran into the tiny convenience store displaying fly-specked girly magazines, cigarettes, milk, and half-priced day-old bread and asked the man sitting behind the cash register if he'd seen a woman in a long skirt get out of his truck.

The man nodded and allowed as maybe he did see a woman, and maybe she was wearing a long skirt, and maybe she did get out of "that there truck." He pointed at Elder Thomas's van, the door hanging open, still parked beside one of the pumps.

"And then right while I'm standin' here, she runs over and jumps right into a car that was just pullin' outta here. But that was a while ago. Didn't see which way they went 'cause I stopped watchin.'"

"When? What kind of car was it?" Thomas's voice was rising, and it was all he could do to keep himself from pounding his fist on the counter.

"Couldn't rightly say how long, mister. Coupla minutes, five, maybe ten?

Like I said, I wasn't lookin' at the clock."

Elder Thomas almost shouted, "Which way did they go?"

The man gave a lazy shrug. "Couldn't say that neither… see, I was watching the TV up there." He pointed to a greasy-looking television set hanging off the opposite wall. "When it's quiet, I like to watch the game shows. I don't pay much attention to what goes on outside unless there's some kinda problem. There weren't no problem I could see. She just got herself outta one car and straight into another one. I figured they was meetin' up. People do that all the time. Hell, done it myself. Drive the wife somewhere, and a friend meets us there, picks her up, and off they go."

By now, the frantic elder could feel the hot flush of anger creeping up his neck toward his face. He punched one fist into the open palm of his other hand.

The man behind the counter waved him down. "Hey, buddy, relax. She'll come back. They always do. Anyways, like I said, she gets into that there other car, and off they go. Didn't want no gas or nothing. Now, I did see that much, mind you. I mean, when they don't get any gas, I do look up. Some folks just stop for gas or a pee or a pack of cigarettes. Sometimes they stop just to get out and stretch their legs. So it wasn't nothing different for her to change cars. People give each other rides here. We're real friendly like."

Elder Thomas was fighting for control and losing the battle. "What color car was the car?"

"Green... blue maybe. Can't remember." The man slowly unwrapped a stick of gum and folded it into his mouth.

"Think, man. Dammit, think. Which way did they go?"

The grizzled man rolled his eyes. "You already asked me that. The road goes both ways, mister, and they went one way or the other. Like I said, I wasn't payin' it too much mind."

The desperate man pulled a scrap of paper and a pencil out of his pocket, scribbled down a telephone number, and shoved it across the counter. "Look. If she comes back, call me. I'll come get her."

The man smoothed it out, set it down in front of the cash register, and smiled. "Sure thing, buddy."

AFTER THE ANGRY CULT GUY STORMED OUT OF THE store, the slow-talking man behind the cash register—the man who couldn't remember anything—straightened up out of his slouch, laughed, and slapped his knee. *Man, oh man*—how he hated those two-faced "Obedient" fuckers. He was a good hardworking Christian man himself, and as much as he didn't hold with lying and swearing and taking the Lord's name in vain, there were times in a day when a man had no choice.

He waited until the van was well away before getting up and opening the door of a supply closet at the back of the store. "You can come outta there now, missy. He's gone."

Obedient Thankful stepped out into the yellow filtered light of the shop and blinked. She looked uncertainly at the man who, without a single question or a second look, had hidden her away and covered for her.

"I uh… I mean… well…" She glanced nervously at the door. "Maybe I could use your phone?"

She started to say more, but he held up his hand and stopped her. "I don't know your name, miss, but I do know where you come from. And if you'll kindly let me, I'll call my wife right now and ask her to come down and talk to you. She knows what to do. Once upon a time, she was one of them lost souls up there herself." He gestured with his thumb in the direction of the compound. "And she did what you just did: saw her chance and hightailed it on outta there. You aren't the first, and I damn sure hope you won't be the last man or woman we'll get out of that holier-than-thou hellhole. Those bastards give my own Lord and Savior, Jesus Christ, a bad name. And speakin' of names, what's yours?"

"Thankful… Obedient Thankful."

"And my name's Cam Spencer." He held out his hand.

"Pleased to make your acquaintance, Miss Thankful. Would you like me to call my wife?"

She nodded and whispered, "Yes, please."

"And how about a nice big bottle of water or maybe some cold milk and one of them ready-made sandwiches in the cooler over there? And then maybe you could do with some chocolate chip cookies. My wife made them fresh this morning. We sell 'em here at the store. They go fast, so be quick."

Chapter Twenty-Eight

❦

Viridienne looked out of the window and squinted in the midday brilliance reflecting off the frozen pond. In her mind, she was already taking the white light, black trees, and electric-blue sky and turning them into a tapestry. Maybe she'd use some glittery yarn and real twigs for visual interest. Her artistic self could feel that lovely tingle in her fingers… *but not now.* Her practical self wisely intervened and told her to go outside and make sure the car would start.

She looked out the front door and smiled. Alison and Fitzpatrick had not only pulled the branch off to the side, but they'd also shoveled out the car and cleared a path to the house. She was good to go. She did a double take. They'd even cleared the feathery snow off the windshield and back window. As long as she backed out slowly and didn't get stuck on a stump or something, she had a clear shot at the ruts in the driveway left by the police car.

However, other than going out, starting the car, and

maybe leave it running and for a few minutes to charge her cell phone, there was no earthly reason to go anywhere and freeze her fingernails off. She had people food, cat food, firewood wood, coffee, wine, and yarn. What she really needed was time to sort out her thoughts—time to be alone with her memories and to feel sad.

Viridienne reached for her knitting basket. When all else failed, the repeated rhythmical movements of knitting calmed her thoughts and soothed her soul. She was beginning to think more clearly. The fact that she was knitting, doing something that felt normal, was a good sign.

Topmost in her mind was Rose's family. She'd never met them but hoped, in honor and memory of her friend, there'd be some way she could be of help. She planned to contact them as soon as she knew they'd been told. But her kindly intentions paled in comparison to the plan she was hatching. One way or another, she would find a way to tell them the truth about Rose's paintings. The way she saw it, the secret artwork—the remaining "missing" pieces she did for the Brandosi family and her own carefully guarded work—was a living part of their daughter and rightfully belonged to them.

As soon as the power came back on, she would use her knowledge of the professional world of fine art and fine-art brokerage to begin an Internet search for the whereabouts and provenance of the paintings of Nicolo Brandosi. She would find out who carried them, what they were selling for, and who owned them. After that, in the guise of a doctoral student doing research on factors affecting the most collected American artists of the last twenty-five years, living or dead, she would start making phone calls. And after that, she would make house calls.

She congratulated herself. It was perfect. No one would suspect anything of a gawky, artsy-looking, midlife graduate student. Women artists, like women doing anything else, were thought to be a lesser breed in the contemporary-art world, and women PhD students weren't even on the scale. She had just woven herself the perfect invisibility cape. *Brilliant!*

There were so many things she needed to know. The first and most pressing was the whereabouts of people who remembered Nicolo Brandosi and his wife, Xenia. Beyond that, she had questions about Rose's life with Nicolo leading up to the night she ran away. And she wanted to know more about Xenia's life before she met her husband… and her childhood and college years.

How much did her family really know? Are there any professors left who might remember her or Nicolo? Is there even more to that horror story than what Rose had told me that night and… at this point, would it do any good to find out?

She took a breath. *Stop right there, Viridienne. Start with the paintings, and don't get ahead of yourself. Take one thing at a time, and each one thing that you uncover will surely lead to the next… or not.*

Viridienne shut her eyes and rubbed the back of her hand across her forehead. She simply could not bring herself to think of her friend as *Xenia*. She was and would always be Rose… and Rose was dead.

Then her mind launched itself into a new unhappy direction: the funeral. She wondered who made the final arrangements for a woman who'd been murdered—a woman who was estranged from her family and who, to all appearances, had a bunch of thugs, somewhere in the shadows, keeping track of her movements.

It was a question for another day and one she probably would not have to answer. She had all she could do to get through this day. But first, she needed to call Detective Fitzpatrick.

FITZPATRICK AND ALISON WERE NEARING HEADQUARTERS on the way back from Viridienne's house when his cell phone went off. He pushed a button and set it on speakerphone. "Fitzpatrick here."

"Um, Detective Fitzpatrick... this is Viridienne Greene calling. I, uh, well... I've been thinking. I wonder if you think it would help if I went with you and Officer Grey when you go to tell Rose's family."

Alison was shaking her head and making the fists-crossed "no" gesture. "Irregular," she mouthed.

"Let me call you back. We're still working out the details." He hung up.

She shook her head a second time. "Totally out of the question."

"Hold on, Alison. If it's against the rules, then there's no question. But if it isn't, I can see how it could be beneficial. Hell, at the very least, she can say something to these poor people that might help. They're about to learn that the daughter they haven't seen in years has been murdered, and the one person who knew her and knew how she lived her life is willing to come and be there when we break the news."

"A woman who could also be a suspect."

"I'd bet my last dollar that she isn't. She may be an artist, and she may look a little bit like a middle-aged gypsy, but she's got a good head on her shoulders. No one could fake her reaction last night—or earlier today for that matter. She's not a suspect."

Alison looked doubtful. "I agree with you there, but until we rule it out completely, don't you think you should at least consider it? Weren't we just talking about personal involvement and professional boundaries?"

"We were. But I'm thinking about the victim's family now. Jaysus, Alison, if it's not against regulations, and even if it is, there's two possible benefits I can see."

"And they are…?" She tipped her head and cocked an eyebrow at her partner.

"First, we get to see Viridienne in a different setting and get an extended time to talk with her. She might be able to add more to what we already know. In fact, weren't we already talking about bringing her in again?"

"Uh-huh…and what's the other benefit?" She was looking only marginally less skeptical.

"With her right there with us—somebody not in uniform —the family might tell us a lot more about their daughter than they would if it was just us talking to them. Think about it."

"You have a point there. Okay, so go find out. Or do you want me to do it?"

He hesitated for a fraction of a second, noting Alison's curious look. "No, that's okay. I'm going to make an executive decision. As the senior officer on the case, I can decide, and I think she should come. I will check the regs just to be sure one way or the other, and I'll let you know."

She shot him a dark look. "So when are you going to call the parents?"

"As soon as I get back to my desk. And right after I do that, I'll call Viridienne and tell her where to meet us. Providence is about an hour and a half from here, maybe two because of the snow."

"So we could be there by three."

"I figure between three and three thirty."

She responded with a thumbs-up.

His voice dropped. "I hate this, you know."

Alison nodded. No words needed. It was the worst part of their job, and they both knew it.

Chapter Twenty-Nine

❦

B ack in her cottage, Viridienne was tearfully poking
around in her ice-cold studio, looking for anything
she might have that had belonged to Rose. DT,
sensing her agitation, was right on her heels and, when he
could manage it, under her feet. For several years, Rose
had made a limited edition of hand-painted Christmas
cards and given them to a few select friends. Viridienne
treasured every single one. The thought of parting with
them was awful, but the idea of not giving them back to
Rose's family was worse. "What do you think, DT? Maybe
I should keep one for myself."

Then she thought about the paintings in the attic of
Rose's house. *How many are there? What will happen to them?
And what will happen when the true story finally gets out—which of
course it will?*

She stopped, straightened up, and clapped both hands
over her mouth in horror. The full impact of Rose's fearful
warning really hit home. The Brandosi family would learn

that she was the one who knew the real story of the paintings and had told it all to the police. *Will they come after me?*

As she made a mental list of questions to ask Fitzpatrick, the house telephone rang. She was picking her way
through the clutter in her studio, so she had to trot into the
kitchen to answer it. Not too many people used landlines
these days, and she was thinking about disconnecting hers
altogether and saving herself a few dollars.

By the time she reached the phone, it had stopped ringing. She stood listening to her own voice telling the caller to
please leave a name and number and a brief message. The
little screen above the touch pad listed the callback number
as "unidentified caller."

Just what I need, she thought, scowling at the phone, *a
goddamn telemarketer*. Like so many of such calls, it disconnected when the recording came on. It rattled her—so
much so that when her cell phone rang within minutes of
the hang up, she was careful to check the caller ID before
pushing the talk button.

"Hi, Viridienne, Detective Fitzpatrick here. I decided
that it probably would be a good idea for you to come with
us to Providence this afternoon. Can you do it?"

She gulped. "Of course. Want me to come in to the
station, or do you want to meet me somewhere along
the way?"

He hesitated. "Actually, it would make things a little
easier if we could meet you somewhere... that is, if you
don't mind. We were planning to come out and pick you
up, but it really would make a difference timewise."

"No problem. Tell me where and when."

"I think we'll take Route 44 all the way. It's a little

slower, but the drive at this time of day will be easier. Can you meet us in a half hour at the commuter parking lot at Exit 5, near the back fence? That's a pretty straight shot for both of us."

"I'll be there."

"Thank you, Viridienne. I appreciate this. It's not going to be easy for any of us, but you being there might be a real help."

Understatement of the year, she thought. "Rose was my friend. It's the least I can do." She paused, fighting for control of her voice. "Thank you, Fitz. See you in a few."

Chapter Thirty

✦❦✦

By midafternoon of that same day, the annual Mayflower midwinter exhibition was fully installed. Every painting, sculpture, and photograph was mounted and labeled, but there was none of the happy satisfaction that usually followed a big job well done. The mood was deeply subdued, and conversation amongst the volunteers was minimal. Even then, they spoke in hushed voices.

"Well, I guess that's it," said Pauline "We've done it. The show is hung, the reception is canceled, and I feel like I've been run over by a truck. A big truck."

Vaughn sighed and nodded. "What do we do now? Go home, I guess. We've notified everyone, refused to talk to anyone connected to the media, closed the gallery for the rest of the week, and put a sign on the door. There's nothing else we can do here." He paused. "Say, did that policeman—I forget his name—say anything about if or when he wanted to talk to us?"

Karen shook her head. "He has our contact information. He's okay. I know his family. They grew up next to us
in Southie. Moved down here same time we did. I'm just
glad he told us not to talk to any of the reporters. Those
guys are like vultures. I suppose they're doing their job, but
they are so in-your-face. Just look out the window. It's cold
as hell, and there they are, waiting for one of us to come
out." She shivered and rubbed her arms.

"Well, what do you expect? Murder is news. But the
last thing I want to do is say something stupid in front of a
TV camera."

"I have an idea," said Bob. "If we all go out together,
we can sort of protect each other."

"I wish I could just throw a snowball at them, you
know, and scare them off. A snowball."

"It is a good idea, Jackson, but let's save the snowball
for another time. You parked close by didn't you?"

"Right out in front. Road's really narrow with the snow
piles. Slippery too."

Bob held up his hand. "Okay, here's what I suggest.
Jackson and I will walk each of you ladies to your cars,
then I'll come back here with Jackson and do a final check
and lock up. I'm parked right behind him."

Lynne shot a grateful look. "Thanks, Bob. That makes
me feel a lot better. I don't mind telling you I'm not feeling
all that strong right now."

"Come on, everybody. Get your coats on. It's time to
go home. I'll shut off the lights and set the alarm." Pauline
shooed everyone along as if they were nervous chickens,
but not one of them squawked.

The sad little band of volunteers came out of the building, and in a single unhappy clump, they pushed past the foot-stamping, frigid reporters, warding off the questions and repeating, "No comment."

Chapter Thirty-One

Viridienne's original plan for the rest of that unhappy afternoon had been to get onto her computer and see what she could find out about the famous Nicolo Brandosi and his darkly influential family. But all that changed when she agreed to go to Providence with Detectives Fitzpatrick and Grey. The Stamos family had been nothing more than vague images that existed in the shadows of her friend's life. The exception was Rose's brother Yanni, who Viridienne knew through descriptions. Now the names and the shadows were about to become real people. She tried to imagine them.

Then she wondered about the Brandosis. *Will I ever meet any of them? Do I want to?* Organized crime was big business, and word had it that there was a significant mob presence in Providence. Beyond that, she knew little more than what she'd learned from news reports and seeing *The Godfather* years before.

She'd never in her life known anyone who could wield

such power… or maybe she had. She shivered and remembered her own family of origin, the Society of Obedient Believers. The leaders, all male of course, were snakes in human bodies—ruthless, all-powerful, demanding total submission, and merciless if their authority was challenged. It was a world where those with the most money and power made the rules and women were little more than useful property—wives, child bearers, and pleasure machines.

Remembering that, she was more committed than ever to bringing the truth to light. And when all of this was behind her, she would begin a dedicated search for her cherished little sister. But all of that would come later. At the moment, she needed to get moving.

She thought briefly about locking the door, and then, in view of the multiple warnings she'd received, she decided to play it safe. She stood with her back to the door and did a visual sweep of the place. None of it had much monetary value, but her home was priceless beyond measure in what it represented. DT was ensconced in her chair, and the woodstove was on *slow but steady*—her term for resting comfortably. With the power blessedly and fully restored, the clock on the wall was ticking, the cable box under the seldom-used TV was blinking, and the refrigerator was humming.

The candles were trimmed and stashed for the next time, and the doors and windows were closed tight and locked against the continuous wind off the pond. She hated the idea of locking the door. This was her safe place… her hideout. The only people who knew about it were the town tax collectors, land officials, and one or two select people at the gallery. Rose, of course, had known. And now, two police detectives did as well. Hardly anyone but the geese, deer, and the foxes came by the house. *Still,* she cautioned herself, *better safe than sorry.* She checked to see that she had the key in her pocket before pulling the door shut hard behind her and setting off. She was not looking forward to the rest of the afternoon—in truth, she was dreading it. But she was alive, and Rose's unsuspecting parents were about to have their world torn apart. Being there for them, helping them however she could was the only thing she could do for Rose.

Outside, the air was clear and cold. She pulled out her sunglasses, which immediately fogged up due to the change in temperature, and climbed into the car. Her venerable, dependable Volvo coughed, sputtered, and started on the second try. She twisted in the seat and, looking over her right shoulder, negotiated a perfect three-point turn in the pristine snow.

One down and two to go. She steered carefully into the ruts left by Fitzpatrick and Alison earlier in the day and headed for the main road. *That's two.* The third challenge would be to get herself to the parking lot at Exit 5 in the time that was left. *I'm good,* she thought. And then she corrected herself. *No, I'm not good. I'm just going to be on time, that's all.*

She made better time than she thought she would and arrived before the old car had even begun to warm up. Freezing, she drove to the far end of the parking lot. She looked around, spotted the black-and-white police car, and pulled up next to it. After locking the Volvo, she climbed into the back seat of the patrol car and immediately tucked her hands inside her cape and up into her armpits. She'd forgotten her gloves, and however unladylike it might look, this was the fastest way she knew to warm her fingers up. *Am I dreaming, or do I smell coffee?*

Alison Grey reached over her shoulder and held out a container of coffee. Viridienne sighed her gratitude, unwound her hands, and reached for it.

"Have you called the parents?"

Fitzpatrick answered, "Just the father and one brother who recently moved back home. He's the one who took the call. The mother has passed away. I just said we had some important information concerning his sister and asked whether they would be home at around five today."

Viridienne was warming her hands on the coffee. "What did they say?"

"What people usually say in such circumstances. They were worried and anxious. They wanted to know what it was we needed to tell them and why we couldn't say what needed to be said over the phone. Don't forget, they knew damned well why she had so little contact with them. It was all part of the agreement. They were keeping her safe, and she was protecting them. That way, nobody talks. Don't ask, don't tell. So of course they're concerned." He made a fist and hit the steering wheel. "I fucking hate this."

Viridienne didn't have to ask what he hated or why he hated it. For a while, they drove in silence. They were well into the city of Taunton before Fitzpatrick spoke again.

He asked her how long she and Rose had been friends and whether there was anything else, however insignificant it might seem, that she could add to the picture before they got to Providence. "Maybe something that might help the parents?"

Viridienne thought hard, pulling up past conversations and little vignettes, mentally going over the different times they were together. It all seemed so fragmented, like shards of broken glass, broken, twisted threads, splinters. She recalled street names, family names, professors' names, and the year Rose graduated from RISD... and the year of her wedding to Nicolo.

A ten-year friendship, and this is all that's left? She had to admit it wasn't much. Rose had been a very private woman, but in the end, that hadn't done her much good. Viridienne felt tears prickling at the corners of her eyes— tears she ordinarily would have fought to hold back. This time, she didn't even try. And when Fitzpatrick, who'd been checking on her in the rearview mirror, passed a folded handkerchief to her over his shoulder, she managed a weak smile and took it.

In other circumstances, Viridienne would have enjoyed the ride. The back-roads route from Plymouth to Providence was very scenic and, in fact, offered a well-illustrated social and economic history of the area. Clustered blue-collar mill towns gave way to more rural smallholdings. Fully restored Victorian homes once owned by early New England industrialists stood next to others from the same period that had been converted to apartments and condominiums. And others, once just as grand, had been abandoned and left for the weeds to devour as they stood in silent witness to the passage of time and social change.

Throughout the trip, Viridienne could not stop thinking about Rose and how she'd died and the unbearable truth that for most of the years of her life, she'd been a victim... and a slave. The life she'd lived had never been her own. The fact that Rose was finally free of the constraints and the fear that had hobbled her offered little comfort, but with every passing mile, Viridienne strengthened her resolve to seek justice.

Alison's voice broke into her thoughts. "How are you doing back there? Are you warm enough?"

"Uh-huh, but thanks for asking. The coffee helped. I know I sound like a broken record, but I still can't believe all of this. Who in the world would do such a thing?"

"That's what we are going to find out, and speaking of that, when we do get to her parents' house, I want you to say nothing until we ask you to. Is that clear?"

Viridienne felt as if she were being chastised before she'd had a chance to do anything wrong.

Fitzpatrick shot a quick look at his partner. "The reason is that those first few minutes when a family learns of this can be critical for getting information. I know that probably sounds heartless to you, and in some ways it probably is, but in the long run, it's good for getting to the core of things—which, in the end, is what we are after."

"I can understand that," said Viridienne, secretly wishing she didn't. Her sense of dread and discomfort was growing with every passing mile. *Why the hell did I say yes to this?* She was wishing that she hadn't made the call to Fitzpatrick suggesting that she come along. *What was I thinking?* She leaned back against the vinyl seat and closed her eyes —not sleeping, just thinking. The daylight around them was fading fast.

"Almost there," said Fitzpatrick over his shoulder. "Remember, now: we do the talking."

"It's possible they may not even want you to come into

the house," said Alison. "There's no script for these things."

Viridienne opened her eyes and watched as Fitzgerald pulled up in front of a substantial-looking brick-fronted home on a wide tree-lined street. She knew she was in Providence but had no idea where.

"Ready?" Fitzpatrick pulled open the door and extended his hand to help her out.

"As ready as I'll ever be."

Chapter Thirty-Two

T he meeting with the Stamos family was not at all what she had anticipated. *But what kind of expectations does one have for such a thing?* When they entered the house, a man who introduced himself as Yanni, Xenia's older brother, took their coats, invited them into the living room, and introduced them to his father, Dimitri. Rose's mother, Ephrosinia, had died earlier that year, and her elderly widower was bent and wearied by loneliness and befuddled by advancing dementia.

Viridienne deliberately seated herself away from the others in a comfortably cluttered living room that must have once been lavishly appointed. She was expecting and dreading an emotional display of grief and anger, but Rose's father and brother were subdued, almost stoic, in their reaction to the news.

Once everyone was seated, Yanni—tight jawed and twisting his fingers—opened the conversation in a harsh whisper. "I always knew they'd get her. It was just a question of when."

Fitzpatrick and Alison jumped on that simultaneously, asking what he meant, but Yanni retreated into generalities.

"Everyone knew that the Brandosi family was connected to the mob, but it was one of those things you never ever talked about—at least, not where you could be heard. The walls have ears around here, and everybody is connected to somebody. You learn to shut up and keep your head down. There was nothing we could do back then. So I'm not really sure how much I can tell you. You know, the code of silence."

When asked, he was adamant that he didn't want to hear the specifics of Rose's death. "It's bad enough to know she's gone," said Yanni. "I don't need to know how it happened."

In the end, the interview was more of a strained and stilted conversation than anything else—an awkward formality. Viridienne felt like a fifth wheel. They didn't want to know how Xenia-Rose had lived away from them. They didn't want to know anything about her friendship with Viridienne. It was as if a room had been closed off years before, and no one wanted to open it and look inside —no one wanted to be swept away and drowned in the river of pain that would gush out. Viridienne found that strange and wondered if their reaction was simply shock or if the Brandosi family held a sword over their heads as well. *Or maybe it is all tragic, humiliating history and best left buried.*

After breaking the news and responding to their first

reactions, the interview fell back on ritual formality. The brother answered "No" or "I don't know" to almost all of the questions. There were moments when the father seemed to understand that his daughter was dead, but Viridienne couldn't be sure.

Did they know where she had been living? Not really. They knew she lived in Massachusetts. Who were her friends? They didn't know. Had she ever mentioned this woman, the one sitting right here in the living room with them, Viridienne Greene?

Yanni turned, looked at Viridienne, and sadly shook his head. "No."

The one question that evoked any kind of reaction was when Alison asked them, what was Xenia like as a child?

"Quiet," said her brother. "Always off by herself, drawing pictures. She was different. She didn't want to play outside with the other kids. She liked school. I mean, well, she never got in trouble or anything." He got up, picked up a family photograph, and handed it to the detectives. "She's the one in the middle."

The father pointed at the picture. "My Xenie. She home from school yet?"

Yanni looked at his father, blinked several times, cleared his throat, and continued with his remembrances. "She was always kind of a loner. We figured it was because all she ever wanted to do was play with her paints and her crayons. Then she went to art school, and we saw even less of her. She was good, though, real good. She got a scholarship and everything. We were so proud of her. Then she met up with that fucker Brandosi, and everything changed. That's what happens when girls get married. It's all about the husband from then on, isn't it? We hated him for taking her away from us." He shrugged. "What can you do? She was in love."

Viridienne said nothing. She knew the rest of the story, and she knew how it ended.

"Can you tell us how things changed after she got married?" asked Alison.

Yanni was becoming emotional. "Right from the beginning, it was *Nick this* and *Nick that*. It's like he took total control of her. She dropped out of school not too long after she married him, and eventually, she just stopped painting altogether. At first, we thought the reason they got married so fast was because she was pregnant. But that never happened. No kids. Probably for the best."

He paused, emotion playing across his face, then continued. "We worried about her but she kept saying everything was fine. She was a wife now, not an artist anymore, and that was… fine. Turns out we had good reason to worry. But what could I do? She'd made her bed and closed the door after herself."

Only she didn't stop painting. Is it possible they don't know the whole story? Do they think that Rose left her husband only because of the abuse? Do they know that he took over her life and her art and did his best to take over her soul? And what did they know about the sudden and unexpected death of Nicolo Brandosi?

The more she listened to Yanni, the faster the questions multiplied in her mind. Maybe there was more to this than she knew… maybe more than even Rose knew. These were questions for another time, and she alone would find the time and place to ask them.

"Here's your cape."

Viridienne blinked. She'd been miles away, following her own thoughts as the tragic mystery continued to twist in on itself.

"Oh. Uh, thank you, Fitz."

She stood and wound herself into the folds of the comforting Irish wool and secured it with the attached scarf that doubled as a hood. It was cold and dark outside, and she pulled the cape more tightly around her as they walked back to the car.

"My grandmother had something like that," said Fitz, pointing to her cape. "She brought it with her when she came over from Ireland."

"I got mine in a secondhand store," said Viridienne. "Would you believe it's from Ireland? Had the tags still on it. Never been worn."

"My grandmother would have loved it," said Fitz.

Chapter Thirty-Three

T he man turned carefully onto the dirt road and, taking care to keep to the previously carved-out ruts, drove slowly to the end. If she was home and saw him, he'd apologize and say he was making a delivery and must have gotten the address wrong. But her car was gone—for how long, he couldn't know, but even if she did come back, the delivery story would work. It always did. *Stick with what you know*, he reminded himself as he crunched to a stop. *And stay in the car.*

He looked at the house then pulled out his phone and photographed the front door, noting the location of the windows, and the orientation of the screen room. Not that he was likely to need it, but one could never be too sure. This was insurance. His mother always said the devil was in the details. It was good advice. He'd always been a detail man, and that had served him well. Just to be sure, he pulled out his cell phone, opened the car, leaned out as far as he could, and in the failing light, snapped a couple of pictures of the surroundings for later reference should it become necessary.

He knew better than to get out of the car. *No footprints.* He pocketed the phone and backed out of the narrow road, once again taking care to stay exactly in the ruts that Viridienne had so conveniently left for him. *Details!* It had been a long time since he'd thought about his mother.

Chapter Thirty-Four

✦❦✦

After concluding the meeting with Yanni and Dimitri, Detectives Grey and Fitzpatrick drove Viridienne back to her car in the commuter lot then stayed beside it until the lights came on and it started. The air was dark and cold, but the roads were clear.

Fitz waited until she was fully out of sight before slipping the patrol car into gear and setting off in the opposite direction. "Your thoughts, Ali?"

"Fitz, you know as well as I do, there's always something they're not saying. Sometimes it's deliberate—sometimes it's the shock of it all. That's why we always make a return trip."

"I suppose. I think we can write off the father—he's pretty out of it with the dementia and all—but the brother might have something more to tell us."

"Think so?"

"I'd lay money on it. Don't you remember? He took an extra beat or two answering a couple of the questions.

That always means they're thinking about what to say. And if they are thinking about what they want to say, they're also thinking about what not to say."

"I guess." She paused. "You know, I wouldn't discount the old man completely. If you can manage to trigger the right memory, you might be able to pick something up."

"I suppose, but I'd have to find the trigger. I'll stick with the brother for now."

"Are you going to question Viridienne again?"

He nodded. "Absolutely. I know you had your doubts, but in the end, I do think it helped having her come along with us. With her there, it wasn't so clinical… so cut-and-dried. You know what I mean?"

"Maybe yes, maybe no," said Alison. "Too soon to tell. On the other hand, she is a living connection to their daughter. She knows about parts of Rose's later life that her parents don't know. If I were the brother, I'd want to talk to her again—without a couple of detectives taking notes. I can see her going back there on her own."

"Jaysus, I hope she doesn't."

"Why so?" asked Alison.

"She didn't say much, but I was watching. She took in every word. She wants to know what happened to her friend. Maybe even more than we do."

"And considering who and what we might be dealing with here, too much poking around could be dangerous to her health."

Fitzpatrick nodded. "That's what worries me. But let's save the rest of this until tomorrow. I need to sleep on this stuff. You know me—I gotta turn it all over in my head a few hundred times. We've got the notes. We've got the tape.

Little Rosie isn't going anywhere. Anything else can wait for the light of day."

"Fitz?"

"Mmm?"

"Did you really get permission from the chief to bring her along?"

Fitz favored her with a quick sideways glance. "Nope."

"You owe me, buddy." She winked.

"I owed you long before this, lady, but you're right... and I'll make good on it."

Alison grinned at her partner and shook her head. "Just kidding. You owe me nada, kemosabe. We're a team. You lie, and I'll swear by it. CYA to the end. Blood brothers."

"But you're a girl. Girls can't be brothers."

"You noticed!"

"I did, but I've heard you swear like a man when you put your mind to it."

"Shall I take that as a compliment?"

Chapter Thirty-Five

Back in the peace, quiet, and warmth of her own home, and far too tired to think about food, Viridienne dropped into her chair like a deflated balloon. Even her bones were tired. *Bone weary.* That was what Rose used to say after a day of painting. *Damn*—she was going to miss that woman.

DT waddled over to her feet and waited to be invited up onto her lap. He was not a pushy cat like some she knew. He always asked permission. She patted her knee, and he obliged. Despite having only one eye and being overweight, DT had not lost the ability to jump, land, curl up, and start purring in one fluid motion. He didn't believe in wasting time or energy. She leaned back in her chair, wiggled her fingers into his belly fur, and felt the tension in her back and shoulders beginning to release. It had been such a long day.

She opened her eyes and looked at the clock on the microwave. It was almost midnight, and her neck hurt

JUDITH CAMPBELL

from sleeping scrunched up on her chair. This was becoming a bad habit. The cat was back on the floor in front of the woodstove, and the temperature in the house had dropped to an uncomfortable level. She shivered, rubbed the kinks out of her neck and shoulders, and stood up. After adding a log to the fire and pulling on one of her signature shaggy sweaters, she powered up her laptop. There was something she needed to do immediately.

An hour later, bleary-eyed but clearheaded, she'd put into place the bare bones of the plan she'd been mulling over. She'd found the one gallery that carried Nicolo's paintings and another smaller, less impressive-looking one in Providence. The big fancy one, Gallery 757, was in New York City. She had an address, a phone number, and the gallery website. With impotent despair no longer clouding her thinking, she shut down her computer, rolled up in the nearest blanket, fell onto the sofa, and slept like a rock.

IN PROVIDENCE, XENIA'S BROTHER HAD BEEN PACING THE floor for hours. The old man had long since gone to bed, and Yanni was alone in the living room of the house he'd grown up in. Little had changed from when they were children. Maybe a few more family photographs on the piano, footstools, and lap robes for older feet and legs. The arms of the chairs were showing their age, and the drapes and curtains had faded where they were exposed to the sun. His mother never would have allowed any of this if she were still alive. Her chair remained empty. Her black knitted shawl still hung over the back. He picked it up and sniffed.

168

It still smelled like her. He rubbed his cheek on the shawl then refolded it and set it back on her chair.

Yanni was of two minds. Part of him wanted to have this over and done with as quickly and quietly as possible—to just close the door on Rose and let it be. Digging up the past could have serious ramifications and could affect everyone. On the other hand, his sister was dead. In some ways, she'd been dead for years—accepting her absence as the new normal was the only way all of them had been able get on with their own lives. But that was then, and this was now, and all bets were off.

He knew the terms of the deal: no contact, nothing that would raise suspicion. And in order to protect her and keep her alive, the rest of the family had agreed to the terms. "Supposedly," they said by way of assurance, "she will be well taken care of."

She would have a nice house and a new identity, and no one would ever be the wiser about who really created those paintings with the name Brandosi scratched in huge bold letters in the lower right-hand corner. But his sister was dead… murdered. And the son of a bitch who'd killed her was walking around out there somewhere, free as a bird. And who was to say all of this didn't have a hand in his mother's early death? She began her decline within the year of Xenia's move.

He stopped midstride and punched his right fist into the palm of his left hand. His mind told him to let sleeping dogs lie. *Don't dig around in the past. What's done is done.* His heart told him his sister, and therefore his whole family, had been grievously wronged. Those mendacious, murderous bastards, the Brandosis, were living off her legacy. But it was not about the money. First, they killed her soul. Then, just two days ago, they finished the job. He literally growled as the ugly truth of it all came fully into focus perhaps for the first time. He would not remain silent, but neither would he go to the police—at least, not yet. This was a family matter. He knew about dealing with family matters, and he also knew it was something you never, ever, talked about. *Blood demands blood.*

Those people meant business, and they had long memories. Whatever he did, he would have to do it in secret until he learned the truth—not the story they'd always told when anyone asked, but the truth about what had really happened to his little sister, the serious little dark-haired girl with the paints and the crayons and a smile —when you could get one out of her—that would light up a whole room. The one who ran to him, rather than her mother, when she was hurt… the one he could no longer protect.

He had an idea. He'd contact that woman who was a friend of his sister—the one who came with the two detectives. *What the hell is her name again? Weird name. Like Vivian, only longer.* He hadn't really been paying attention. *French sounding. Viridienne, that's it. Not too many artists with that name in southeastern Massachusetts—or anywhere else, for that matter.*

She'd be easy to find. Yanni was good at finding what he wanted. The one thing he would not do was call the Plymouth police to get her name. That would be way too much information in the wrong hands. No point in involving them. This was family business.

Chapter Thirty-Six

Viridienne slept late the following morning—a deep, honest, untroubled sleep. By noon, in the bright light of midday, she was up, dressed, and seated with the sun on her back at her table by the window. She was doing a second, wider Internet search on Nicolo Brandosi, the phenomenally talented artist from Rhode Island who'd died so young and so tragically in a freak accident at the peak of his career. Questions would always remain. Like Icarus, had he flown too close to the sun? Did the fame and the fortune and the drugs and the alcohol finally get to him? And if not that, then what had happened?

She clicked and browsed and searched. Then, doubling back and rechecking her notes, she created a Word file with anything relevant she could find. It was depressingly clear that Rose hadn't told her half of it. The tangle Viridienne was discovering was darker than anything she had ever considered in her worst imaginings.

One piece of information led to the next until the piercing ring of the telephone jangled her back into the present. She fumbled for the phone.

"Hello?"

"Is this Viridienne Greene?"

Oh, God, not more bad news, she thought. "This is Viridienne."

"This is Yanni Stamos. I'm Xenia's brother. We met when you came to my house yesterday."

DT was hungry and knocking loose items off the coffee table to get her attention. She nudged him with her foot with a silent promise of sustenance in the not-too-distant future. The persistent animal was not amused.

"Of course, Yanni. Sorry if I sound fuzzy. I was working on… something. How can I help you?"

"I have no right even asking you this, but could we meet up somewhere? I didn't tell the police everything yesterday because I didn't think it was any of their business. My father's old, and his memory isn't so good, but he never knew the half of what really happened. You were my sister's friend for the ten years that we had no contact with her. I know stuff they don't know, and I think maybe you do too. So help me God—" His voice broke. "I'm gonna find the SOB that killed my sister if it's the last thing I do… and I'm thinking—hoping maybe—that you might be able to help."

Viridienne was now on full alert, and she didn't have to think about the answer. "Yes. Where? I live in Plymouth. Is there someplace that's halfway between us?"

"There's a Dunkin' Donuts in a crappy little strip mall in Seekonk, on the Rhode Island border. It's right out there on the main road and about as everyday inconspicuous as you can get."

"I can do that. When were you thinking?"

"I know it's short notice, but are you free this afternoon?"

She paused. "Sure." In truth, going outside was the last thing she wanted to do, but the prospect of getting some information was the deciding factor.

They agreed on a time, and he gave her an address she could tap into her phone for directions. She had half an hour to feed the cat, eat something, and go over notes from the previous night. First things first: she saved the file and emailed it to herself as an added precaution. Then she fed the cat. She'd eat a banana in the car and, if she was still hungry, have something more at the Dunkies.

It was only on the way to her car that she stopped midstride and asked herself what in hell she was doing heading out alone to meet a man she didn't really know to talk about his murdered sister. Viridienne knew about lost sisters. Her heart had never stopped aching for little Thankful, who was surely a grown woman by now. She wondered what kind of a woman she'd become. Maybe after Rose's murderer was found, Viridienne would go back to California and see if she could find her sister... but in truth, she was still terrified of going anywhere near the compound. They might recognize her and drag her back.

She realized, as she squinted into the low winter sun, that this terrible event—the murder of her friend—might also be the very thing that would push her into an active search for her sister. Internet technology had become so much more sophisticated. Heck, if she stayed on the right side of Fitzpatrick, he might be even be able to help pinpoint some places she could look. *But will I ask him?* As a rule, she kept personal things pretty close to the chest. Involving anyone else might be a reach too far.

The car in front of her turned left without warning. Viridienne slammed on the brakes and cut hard to the right. When her brain cleared and the adrenaline level dropped, she took several deep breaths and refocused her attention on the task at hand and the road ahead. It was entirely possible that Yanni Stamos knew more about the death of Nicolo Brandosi than anyone suspected. Fitzpatrick and Grey weren't at all interested in that piece of history. But to Viridienne's way of thinking, there might well be a connection, direct or indirect, between Brandosi's death and Rose's.

She shivered, half in cold and half in fear, and asked herself once again: *What in God's name am I doing?*

Then she started talking herself back down. She was meeting the man in a public place, and she had Fitz's number in her cell phone. She'd take her chances. Viridienne Greene wasn't born yesterday. No—she was born years ago, the night she turned eighteen and ran off into the night.

Chapter Thirty-Seven

"Entered into rest. January 14, suddenly at home, Plymouth resident and artist Rose Doré. Private arrangements are incomplete at this time."

THE MAN WHO STAYED IN THE SHADOWS FOUND THE PRO forma obituary online in the Old Colony Memorial, the local biweekly paper for the town of Plymouth and surrounds. He'd been waiting and watching for it. If the funeral was going to be held in a church, he might actually go. Doing so would be a ritual dotting of the final *i* and crossing the final *t*. It would probably be held in Plymouth. He was certain no one there would have any idea who he was. He wouldn't go in. He'd just stand outside on the street, a curious passerby.

Then maybe I can finally get on with my life.

Chapter Thirty-Eight

The agreed-upon meeting place was nestled in the very middle of a down-at-the-heels five-store strip mall on the Rhode Island-Massachusetts border. Viridienne was still questioning her sanity for agreeing to meet a virtual stranger in a town she'd barely heard of. *Seekonk*—an Indian name, no doubt. Other than its proximity to Providence, Seekonk appeared to have little to recommend it, the kind of town you drove through on the way to somewhere else. Still, a popular coffee shop on a busy roadway was a good bet. There was safety in numbers. She'd read that somewhere.

"You have reached your destination. It is on your left."

Viridienne politely thanked the lady in her GPS, parked way off to the side, and once out of the car, followed the irresistible smell of freshly baked doughnuts. She spotted Yanni the minute she walked through the door. He was sitting at a table along the left wall facing the entrance and got to his feet the moment he saw her come in. She was almost a head taller than he was. In reality, she was a head taller than most of the men she knew, if she bothered to notice, which she rarely did. Her distrust of men, all men, was deep and justified, and her well-above-average height served to keep them at bay. Since leaving the compound, she held herself at a polite and courteous distance from all men. *Maybe someday,* she'd say to herself, but that day never seemed to come.

Yanni's Greek heritage was handsomely obvious in his olive skin, dark curly hair, and five-o'clock shadow. The creases around his mouth and beside his eyes gave a hint of his age. She'd been too distracted the day before to really notice any of this. Now, taking a good look, she thought that all he'd need would be a black fisherman's cap, and he could play a part in one of her favorite movies, *Never on Sunday*. She stifled the impish thought and returned to the business at hand.

Other than an older man in a red plaid jacket who was curled around a cup of coffee at the far end of the lunch counter and a younger man in a backward baseball cap sitting nearer the door, they had the place to themselves. With two cups of industrial-strength coffee on the table between them and a cinnamon bagel with cream cheese for Viridienne, she and Yanni proceeded with caution.

After thanking her for coming, Yanni wasted no time in getting right to the point. "Last night, you told me you were friends with my sister for ten years."

She nodded and swallowed a piece of bagel. "Give or take a few months."

"How did you meet?"

Viridienne related the story of connecting with Rose at

the Mayflower Artists and Artisans. She told him how two single women, focused solely on their art and living as outsiders by choice, discovered they had much in common. Viridienne was the more outgoing of the two though still cautious. Rose was more introverted. It made for a good balance.

She told Yanni that only after she'd known Rose—she simply couldn't think of her as Xenia—for almost seven years did she learn the tragic reason behind the move to Plymouth and her fanatical privacy regarding her art. She told him that the fact that Rose had allowed her to see the paintings at all was a miracle. Maybe Rose had figured she'd been in the shadows and played by the rules for long enough that she could have one trusted friend.

Viridienne took a sip of her coffee and leaned in toward the man sitting across from her. "Before she started bringing anything into the gallery, she made sure no one would ever take photographs of her or her work or make any mention of her in the media. Once she had that part in place, she began to display her own work. Just there. Nowhere else."

"I wonder how they found out," he asked then half answered his own question. "I can only think those bastards down here were keeping track of her, trolling her. She was worth millions to them… but alive and cranking out paintings for them. Not dead. It doesn't make sense."

She nodded. "I can't begin to imagine how they found her, unless someone posted something on Facebook or Instagram or something. You know, a tourist maybe? Plymouth is full of them in the summertime. They take pictures of everything."

"Tell me about it. Providence isn't much better, especially in the summer." He paused and changed direction. "Say, have you ever been to WaterFire in Providence? It's a summer arts event on the river, right in the middle of the city. You should do it sometime. It's really nice. Maybe when all of this is behind us, you could come down sometime, and I can show it to you. It would be something good and beautiful after all this ugliness."

Viridienne's eyes prickled, and her chin quivered. In that moment, in Yanni's face and voice, she saw Rose's enthusiasm and intensity. She closed her eyes and pushed away the feelings that threatened to undo her on the spot.

"You haven't seen her new paintings, have you? She actually managed to change her style. It's like she was two different people—the woman who painted her dead husband's paintings and the Rose I knew, who painted for herself. That woman was bright and dramatic but mysterious at the same time. Her new work was even better than the other stuff." Viridienne stopped and rubbed at her eyes. "I still can't believe she's gone."

"Neither can I." He made a fist and ground it into his other hand with a savage twisting motion. "Jesus. Here I am, having a cup of coffee and waiting to hear when my sister's body will be released so we can plan the..." His voice broke. "Funeral." He pulled out a handkerchief and wiped his eyes. "And all that arrangement stuff is going to fall to me. My father is past it, and my other two brothers are much older and don't live anywhere near here. I told them, of course, right after you all left last night. They'll come in for the funeral, but they didn't know her like I did. We were closer in age. It was almost like two families: the first two boys, then eight years later me, and a few more years after that, Xenia. She was a midlife surprise to everybody. Most of all, my parents." He winked. "At age fifty, the old man was still going strong."

At that moment, Viridienne made the decision to trust Yanni. "What was she like before she came to Plymouth? What was she like as a little girl?"

"I should probably start at the beginning. There were really two Xenias. The first one was my baby sister. She was born when my mother was almost fifty. She was everybody's miracle baby. My parents were not ready for an infant at that stage of life, so we all pitched in—me most of all. I was ten when she was born, and I couldn't get enough of her. My two older brothers were into sports and cars and girls by then and wanted nothing to do with a baby, especially a girl baby. I wasn't interested in any of that stuff yet, so I was the big-brother protector and almost nanny."

Viridienne smiled at the image forming in her mind. "And then what?"

Yanni blinked several times. "She grew, always with a crayon or a pencil and later a paintbrush in her hand. Never liked dolls or playing house. Because she was so much younger than the rest of us, I suppose she was really like an only child. We loved her of course, but she often preferred to be off by herself."

Viridienne nodded. She had been much like that herself when she was little. But for her, it was bits of yarn and string and shiny buttons if she could find them— things she picked up on the street or pulled out of wastebaskets. These she assembled into secret creations and hid away from the others—until the day they were discovered in the sewing room of the compound... and burned in front of her.

She pulled herself back into the present. "When did it all change?"

"When she made the decision to go on to college. It took everything she had to talk my parents into letting her go to art school. They were very traditional. You know, Greek women stay home and remain virgins until they get married, and then they have babies. Men go to work, and if they're rich or lucky, they go to college. All three of us brothers went to college. But I'm getting off track."

He stopped and took a sip of his coffee. "Remember, my mother was over sixty by then, and my father was two years older than her. They did the best they could, but he was getting old, and it was all too much for them. It's like they had no fight left."

"So it was then that she met Brandosi?"

"She told you his name?"

Viridienne nodded. "Of course."

"Wow, she must have trusted you."

"We'd both had a lot of wine one night. I told her my story too."

"So when did it all change?" If Yanni was interested in what Viridienne's story might be, he had the courtesy not to ask.

"Her junior year at RISD. That's when they met, and the rest isn't history, Viridienne—it's a fucking tragedy. Uh, sorry about the f-bomb."

Viridienne waved the apology away. "She told me it started with her finishing up his homework every now and then. But before long she was doing all his work and signing his name."

"The bastard knew when he had a good thing. She was so naïve. He married her as fast as he could—and after that, she pretty much disappeared from sight. Oh, she said it was because she was too busy keeping house. But Viridienne..." He pounded his fist on the table. "From the beginning, she was like a prisoner. He watched her like a hawk. They lived in a three-room apartment in her in-laws' house, a big Victorian at the end of Benefit Street. It was ten minutes' alk to our parents' house. It got so bad that he didn't even want to let her come home for Christmas or Easter. Easter is really big for Greek families. She was a prisoner... his prisoner. I wanted to kill him... but I didn't. It seems that fate did us all a favor and took care of it for us. But I'm getting ahead of myself."

"She told me it got so bad she finally ran away."

"Yeah. She made it all the way to my house. Two miles away. But when I tried to call the cops on him, she started to cry and said he didn't mean it. Begged me not to. You know the typical bullshit. 'He had a bad day. He was upset.' She said, 'I must have done something to upset him.' I can only imagine what he did to her. But the bastard knew better than to do too much damage. She was his bread and butter. She went back that same night."

Viridienne winced at the brutality of it. There was more, but there was no point in telling Yanni. He couldn't have prevented it, and there was nothing to be gained by telling him now.

"How did her husband die?" she asked. Rose had told her about the incident, but she wondered if there was more to it. Yanni might have a different version. If so, the truth might lie somewhere between the two.

Yanni continued. "She found him dead in the Jacuzzi. At first, they thought he'd fallen and drowned. The autopsy determined that somehow, he'd hit the back of his head, fallen into the water, and drowned. But what was it that made him fall? Heart attack, stroke, drug overdose, all of the above? None of the above? He was well-known to be a heavy drinker and a cokehead. His death was officially listed as a heart attack brought on by an accidental over-dose. Case closed."

Yanni snorted in disgust. "He probably borrowed money from the wrong loan shark or told a family secret to the wrong person. Some people are very good at making a death look accidental… if you know what I mean. They hit and run and never get caught. This was a flat-out hit job if I ever saw one. Of course, everybody thought my sister had something to do with it. Some people still do. The bastards."

Chapter Thirty-Nine

Viridienne was having trouble taking this in. She'd known a different kind of evil in her life, but nothing like this. Her coffee had long since cooled, but a kindly, attentive waitress silently removed it and replaced it with a fresh cup. Viridienne smiled in gratitude, and holding up the cup with both hands, she closed her eyes and inhaled.

Yanni broke into her thoughts. "To be honest, I don't really give a shit how Brandosi died. The cops will look for her murderer, and more than likely, they'll find him. It's their job, but that's really only a part of the picture. I want to find out *why* they killed her. It doesn't make sense to kill the goose that lays the golden egg."

Viridienne had no response. The whole thing was spinning out of control. Maybe she should leave it all to the police and the warring families and get out while she still could... or maybe not.

Yanni fiddled with his spoon. "It's partly about the art

and why my sister is dead, and that's bad enough. But think about it: those fucking Brandosi bastards have her paintings—with his name on every goddamn one of them. He really killed her years ago." Once again, he fought for control. "She needs her name back. Xenia Stamos—she's the world-famous artist, not him. It's the least I can do for her."

Viridienne bit her lip and nodded. "I'll do anything I can to help, Yanni. I want the same thing. She was an incredible artist. The paintings need to be out there with her name on every single damn one of them. That's why I agreed to meet you today."

He shook his head and held up a restraining hand. "Uh-uh. You need to stay out of this. These guys play mean and dirty. By meeting here with me, you've already done everything you can. You were her friend when nobody else could be... not even me. For your own safety, you need to go back to Plymouth and stay there. I may need to call you, but other than that, no more meetings. Cooperate any way you can with the police, but don't tell them about talking to me. The Brandosis and their kin have eyes and ears everywhere, and they don't let anything get in their way... at least, not for very long. They are going to go after the paintings that are still in the house. It's just a question of when. Jesus Christ, Viridienne, stay away from that house. I don't want you going anywhere near there."

Even though there was no one close enough to hear her, Viridienne dropped her voice. "Yanni, there's at least another thirty or forty paintings locked in the attic. She took me up there and let me see them, but only once."

"We need to get them out of there."

She grabbed his arm. "What are you talking about? You won't be able to get near the place. The police have it roped off—or whatever they do. It's a crime scene. You know, yellow tape and stuff. I didn't tell them I had a key, but there's no way in hell they'd ever let me in there right now while they're still investigating her death."

"You've got a key?"

"I do."

He looked down at his watch. "Look, I need to get back to my father before he goes out looking for me. He'll do that—go out and wander around on the street if he can't find me. Like I said, I have your number. I'll call you when I've had time to think it all through."

"Yanni?"

He looked up at her. "Mmm?"

"Please let me help."

He shook his head, his mouth set in a firm, straight line. "Uh-uh. Too dangerous. I know how to reach you if I have to…" He stopped and frowned.

"What's the matter?"

"Somebody is going to try to get into that house of hers, and that somebody, surer than shit, will know who killed my sister."

"What are you going to do?"

He shook his head. "I don't know yet. Uh… look, you'd better get going. I will stay in touch, but I'll be very careful when I do. You know what they say—*don't call me, I'll call you.* These are some very bad people we're dealing with here, Viridienne, and they don't let anything or anyone get in their way. Let's just say I've had dealings with them in the past, and I know a lot more about the backstory than I'm telling you. I don't want you turning into collateral damage... because you could. I know how they operate."

That got her attention. "I hear you, Yanni, and thank you. Hands off. I promise."

He smiled, reached across the table, and took her hand. "In Greek family culture, if you help one member of the family, you help all of us. And if you help all of us, it makes you family. You helped my sister. You loved her like she was your own sister. That alone makes you family, but you did way more. Now I gotta protect you too. So stay out of this. I'm the big brother—I do the dirty work, okay?"

The words *family* and *sister* went to the very center of Viridienne's heart,

and the pain was unbearable. She bit her lip and looked away. *Maybe one day, I will tell him.*

"Hey, Viridienne, what's the matter? What are you crying for? What'd I say?"

"Nothing you said, Yanni. One day, I'll tell you—I really will. It's too long a story for right now." She paused, offering him a weak smile. "Meanwhile, I guess we both have our work cut out for us."

"Hold on a minute. What do you mean? We just agreed I'm doing the work in this thing."

She shook her head and held up her hand. "No, no, not that. I have to go back and try to pick up my life. Rose was such a big part of it. It's gonna be really hard not to have her around to bounce things off of. We did that all the time, artist to artist. We helped each other solve design problems and color dilemmas."

Yanni looked both mollified and confused.

"You can't make art in a vacuum," she continued. "You need someone to talk to who understands and speaks the language. Rose and I did that for each other…" Viridienne bit her lip and squeezed her eyes shut.

Yanni reached for her hand again, and this time, he held onto it.

"Thanks," she said. "Anyway, that's what I meant. I'll leave the detective work to the police professionals and the family work to you, and I'll take one day at a time when it comes to getting back to my work."

"Good."

"Oh, geez, I just thought of something."

"What's that?" he asked.

"I'm going to have to go back into her house anyway."

"Why?"

"One of the detectives talked about it. Since I was her friend, I think they thought I might be able to answer some more questions for them. That, and of course, I know where she kept the paintings… his and the ones she did for herself."

Yanni straightened up and leaned forward, speaking with new intensity. "Viridienne, before you go in there with the police, I want to go through it myself… maybe with you." He paused. "That means soon. I want to see things the way she left them. I want to see what's left of her life before strangers dig through it."

She looked straight into his eyes with complete comprehension. "I'll find a way to do that with you." She looked at the clock then out of the window. "Yikes… I need to get going. It's later than I thought."

"I'm sorry. I should have paid more atten—"

She interrupted him with a lift of her hand and began gathering her things. "Don't be silly. It's time, that's all. You've given me a lot to think about. Let me sleep on it, and I'll see what I can do about getting you into the house."

Chapter Forty

Yanni Stamos walked Viridienne to her car and waited while she backed out of the parking space, shifted, clunked into first gear, and turned out onto the main road. When she was out of sight, he got into his own car, a black Mazda Miata—low, lean, and sometimes dangerously fast. Then he left, turning in the opposite direction.

The man, sitting across the parking lot in the nondescript vehicle, watched until they were both out of sight before starting his own car. He'd hit a triple. He had clear pictures and the make, model, and license-plate numbers of both cars.

He left the parking lot, tapped a request into his GPS, and set off at a moderate speed in the same direction as Viridienne had gone just five minutes earlier. Before long, he had her in his sights once again.

Chapter Forty-One

Once the search for the murderer was well underway and in the professional hands of Detectives Fitzpatrick and Grey, and the personal-vendetta search for the mob connections was in Yanni's relentless hands, Viridienne was on her own. Some days earlier, she'd made it her mission to locate the other so-called Brandosi paintings and, when the murderer was safely behind bars, pull back the curtain of secrecy and credit them to the woman who'd actually painted them.

Viridienne was using the hour-plus drive home to clear her head and to work out her own plan—and as part of that, construct her new identity as a myopic hyperfocused PhD student. She'd learned in her preliminary Internet search that most of Brandosi's work could be found at the Gallery 757 on Madison Avenue in New York City and a subsidiary, Gallery 57, located near RISD in Providence. She would make personal visits to both… but she was getting ahead of herself.

The idea was to make the initial contact by email, introducing herself as Valerie something or other and stating the reason for the contact and the nature of her research. With luck, she'd get a response. If not, she would follow up with a phone call. And if that didn't produce anything, she'd get on a train and show up early on a Monday or a Tuesday right after they opened. Early in the week, during winter, the number of visitors and prospective customers was likely to be low, and she would have more time and a better chance of making her case.

As she drove along—she did some of her best thinking while driving—her plan expanded. She would tell the gallery manager she was writing a book and would, with their permission, include the name, address, and contact information of the gallery... and of course, some pictures. She might have had a sheltered childhood, but she'd been out in the real world long enough to know that flattery worked—especially when paired with free advertising. For the first time since Rose's death, she was feeling hopeful. Maybe she could do something. Never one to back down from a challenge, she unconsciously pressed down on the gas pedal as the plan in her head began to expand and take shape.

ON HIS WAY BACK HOME TO PROVIDENCE, YANNI WAS working out a very different plan. He'd known all along that his brother-in-law's death was no accident. He also had a pretty good idea of who'd done it or paid to have it done. He knew a hit job when he saw one. But before he could deal with that, he needed to attend to the details of his sister's final arrangements.

He punched the steering wheel and forced back a sob. *Final fucking arrangements.* He could do final arrangements, all right. And then, by God, when his sister was laid to rest, he'd do just that. One or two other... final arrangements.

Much as he would have preferred to work alone, he knew he'd have to consult with his other two brothers about the funeral. He was of two minds about what kind of funeral to have. On the one side was a small private family funeral, or even maybe just a graveside service, with an Orthodox priest in attendance. To all appearances, that would close the chapter on Xenia's life... except that he would use the finality and the silence to dig into the muck of the Providence underworld until he could trap and catch the river rat who'd killed his sister.

In contrast to the small private service he would have preferred, the other brothers could decide to have a pull-out-all-the-stops Greek funeral with a newspaper article —*or maybe even put something on* 60 Minutes, *for God's sake*— exposing the whole filthy truth about who'd really done the paintings. If they went in that direction, he would be putting a Kill Me sign on his own back. But when they came for him—and they would—he would be waiting. Using himself as bait would be a way to trap the river rats. But before making either type of funeral arrangement, he needed to find out when her body would be released by the medical examiner.

And then his thoughts turned to Viridienne. He smiled,

and his dark mood lightened. What a nice lady she was and pretty in her own lanky way. *Poor thing.* She was grieving too. Whatever they decided to do for a funeral, private or public, he would invite her. After all, she was family now. He smiled. Maybe something good would come out of this awful mess after all.

Chapter Forty-Two

Obedient Thankful stood watch at the door while the man behind the counter called his wife. Even in her distracted state, she couldn't help but notice that his speech was no longer lazy and slurred.

"Hey there, wife lady, I think I got some good news for you. I got a young woman here who just escaped from the compound."

He paused, listening.

"Yup. Jumped out of the truck when the guy driving it went for a pee. She tried to get into a car that was just pulling out, but they drove off. Didn't even open the window, the bastards! Anyway, she ran in here looking like a scared cat, askin' if she could hide somewhere. I got her into the stock pantry just as that SOB come 'round the corner wanting to know if I'd seen her… and all of a sudden, I got real stupid."

Frightened though she was, Thankful began to giggle.

"Told that big ugly dude that I just sit here and watch

TV all day. You know, the game shows. I never know who comes and goes around here, and I couldn't care less. I sell gas, girly magazines, and cigarettes and collect the money." He rolled his eyes.

By that point, Thankful was laughing out loud.

"Anyway, darlin', like I said, I got us a live one here. Looks just like you did when you took off outta there. Half scared rabbit, half deer in the headlights. She said she might be willin' to come stay with us for a bit. You wanna come on down and talk with her?"

He smiled and gave Thankful an energetic thumbs-up.

"I knew you would, darlin'. Ten minutes, give or take?" He nodded and hung up. "I think we have liftoff." He held out his hand to Thankful.

Thankful flinched and backed away.

"Oh, jeez. I forgot. No contact with the opposite sex unless you're married. My wife told me all about that crap. It'll take you a while to get normal after all you been through. Don't worry. We got time. We've helped three others outta there before you come in here—two girls and a guy. Talk about a horror show." He paused. "Will you listen to me—I'm yakkin' away like a motorcycle in full throttle. You eat your sandwich, and I'll straighten things up around here. My wife tells me I talk too much. Guess I do."

Thankful smiled and bit into her sandwich. She was beginning to relax.

"I got a chair back here if you want to sit down. My wife, her name's Donna. She got herself outta there some ten years ago, and we met up, and she stuck around. We got four kids now. And after all that time, some little bitty thing can still set her off. What do they call it? PTSD or something. All I know is that if everything she told me is true, then you, little lady, have been through hell, and you've just done about the bravest thing in your whole life. My hat's off to you, and—well, looky there." He pointed toward the door. "Here comes Donna. Right on time, God bless her. Don't tell her I've been talkin' your ear off, or she'll give me what for." He winked, and Thankful smiled for the second time that day as Donna Spencer came in through the open door with one child on her hip and another holding onto her hand. She was wearing jeans and a shirt that was so oversized it looked like it was wearing her instead of the other way around.

"Mama's got the other two back home. I figured we might need some room in the car." She held out her hand. "Hi, my name's Donna. It used to be Verity when I was in there—you know, it means truth… what a joke that was. I changed it as soon as I could. What do we call you?"

This time, Thankful took the extended hand and said, "They named me Obedient Thankful, so… call me Thankful… for now."

"Thankful it is, then—for now, anyway." Donna had a face that anyone would love with wide-open light-brown eyes. Her light-brown curly hair was pulled back in a ponytail, and she had strong, powerful hands. The two children looked just like her.

"Cam here probably told you that I escaped out of that hellhole ten years ago. He found me hiding in a state park, sneaking food from campsites when the residents went out. He was a ranger there. Anyway, he brought me home to his mother, who knew all about the society. She found me a family to stay with through her church." She paused and smiled. "I guess you could say the rest is history, and it is, but Cam took his time. He knew I'd been through the mill. Now look at me. Fair, fat, and forty with four kids and not counting anymore." She shot a warning glance at her husband, and they both laughed.

She continued. "Anyway, things were good, and they kept getting better. I decided my way of giving back was to help people like you—and like me—however we could... and here comes you runnin' in the door. Right on time."

At that point, Cam went outside to help a customer at the gas pump. Donna went on with her story, explaining how, if Thankful was willing, she could stay with them for as long as she wanted to and help out in the house and the garden when she felt up to it. "*Not* slave labor, mind you," said Donna emphatically, "but just like the rest of us. Family. We all do our bit."

Thankful nodded. She was feeling comfortable with this kindly woman.

"Like I said, you can stay as long as you want. It takes some people longer than others to get used to being outside of there. You gotta learn all kinds of new stuff."

"We had a computer in the compound. The women weren't allowed to use it, but when everybody was out and I was supposed to be cleaning the offices, I learned a little bit. Then I learned a little bit more. I wanted to try looking for my sister, but I still didn't know enough for something like that. Besides, I was afraid someone would catch me."

"You have a sister?"

Thankful nodded. "Obedient Charity... that was her name before she ran off. She hid a note in my jacket pocket the night she left. It said that if I ever wanted to find her, she would be as far away as she could get and she would change her name to something that had the name of a color in it, but she didn't say which one. I have it with me." Her voice caught. "It's all I have left, and it's sure not much to go on, but it's how I carry my hope. I don't even know if she's still alive, but somehow, I need to believe she is."

"I'm sure she is, and I promise I'll do what I can to help you find her. So now I'm asking: will you come home with us?"

Thankful nodded as Cam, all smiles, came back into the store and took up his spot behind the register. "Well, look at you two. Family already."

Donna waved him off. "Not so fast, you. This is gonna take some time. She'll be family when and if she's ready and not a minute sooner. I know you mean well, but sometimes, you can trip over your own big fat heart."

Cam regrouped and did a little mock bow. "So, Miss Thankful, might you consider comin' home and stayin' with us for a spell?"

Donna laughed and smacked him on the shoulder. "I already asked, and yes, she's coming."

They were so involved with getting to know one another that not one of them saw or heard Elder Thomas walk into the store. It was one of Cam's kids who looked past them all and said, "Daddy, I think you got a customer."

Elder Thomas was standing just inside the door, feet apart, arms half-raised, ready to make a grab for Thankful if she tried to escape.

In a nanosecond, Cam was out from behind the

counter and inches from the man's face. "She ain't goin' nowhere with you, you sanctimonious two-faced son of a bitch. You lay one hand on her, and I'll take your balls off right here and now, one at a time, and it won't be quick. Sorry, ladies. So you get your ass on outta here, and don't you ever come back. Not for gas, not for a piss, not for a free day-old loaf of bread. Get out!" Spittle was collecting at the corners of his mouth, and he wiped savagely with the back of his arm. "Get out."

Elder Thomas jerked his head toward the door. "Come on, Thankful. Get in the car. I won't tell."

Thankful, hardly breathing, shook her head slowly from side to side and stood her ground. "I'm staying here."

Chapter Forty-Three

O ver the weekend, after a long, argumentative meal and several bottles of retsina topped off with cloudy glasses of ouzo, the three Stamos brothers came to a compromise agreement regarding their sister's funeral. It would be held in their family church, but the service itself would be by invitation only, and the final interment would take place later in the year, when the ground was thawed and they could open a grave. The ceremony itself would take place as soon as they could retrieve her body, and nothing of the arrangements would be made public.

As the plan for locating the "Brandosi" paintings unfolded, Viridienne decided that Valerie Stone would be her grad-student name. It was near enough to her own name that she'd remember to answer to it as well as not forget it when someone asked. She would make the first gallery inquiry the next morning, and for the time being, she would keep this particular investigation to herself. After all, she wasn't looking for the killer—she was looking for the paintings. If her investigation into the paintings led her to information about the killer, then she'd call Detective Fitzpatrick. But the first order of business would be getting her foot and her face through the doors of both galleries—the one in New York and the smaller one in Providence.

She waited until Monday to make the first call, and as it turned out, she had no problem at all contacting the New York Gallery directly. After two rings, a pleasant-sounding woman picked up the phone, thanked her for calling, and asked the reason for the call. After introducing herself as Valerie Stone, a graduate student in art history, Viridienne stated that her interest was not in purchase but in research. She asked if she could come in sometime soon and simply look at the Brandosi paintings and learn more about them firsthand.

"Thank you for calling, Valerie. My name's Stella Van Daam. I'm the gallery manager. We've had a lot of interest in the Brandosi pieces lately. Like anything else, interest in a name or a genre in the world of art seems to ebb and flow over time, but the Brandosi work always holds its place. Highly collectible, and desirable, especially because he died more than ten years ago, when he was still a rising star, and there were so few of them left on the market."

"I understand several more have turned up since he died. That's amazing,"

Viridienne was speaking as Valerie Stone, the very

essence of eager academic-sounding innocence. "I wonder if they'll find any more."

"Ah... I can only hope. People keep finding lost or hidden Rembrandts and Picassos, so there's no reason why a few more Brandosis wouldn't turn up on the scene. You know, those amazing finds from church rummage sales and garage sales.

"I'm sure you've seen *Antiques Roadshow*. Finding the hidden masterpiece is every collector's dream. But we are getting off the subject."

"As I understand it, you are doing research on the top ten most recognized American artists, living or... uh, dead. What exactly are you researching? I mean sales and prices are a very small part of the picture... if you'll pardon the pun."

Viridienne was prepared. "Agreed. It's no news to you that names, schools of art, and even sizes of art can trend up and down. I am trying to find out what has influenced the trends in one way or another since the start of the millennium. That's a fairly small window when you think about it."

"I'll be very interested in what you learn. Yet we both know that some artists' work never loses value. I'm thinking of someone like Andrew Wyeth or Pablo Picasso or Ansel Adams. Their work is timeless."

"That's it in a nutshell," said Viridienne. "What makes one piece timeless and another a passing fad? In ten- or twenty- or fifty-years' time, will the artists that I am researching be timeless? Will their work hold its value... or not?"

"I think people in the art world have been asking that

question ever since there was an art world. Do you know that some really wealthy collectors, many of them Asian and Eastern European, will buy up a body of work and then store it away in a huge vault just so it can appreciate in value? It's not on display—it's just hidden away, supposedly making money. What a waste. I'd hate to think of the Brandosi pieces locked up somewhere."

Funny you should say that.

"I'm thinking of Vermeer and his thirty-four or thirty-six paintings, depending on who's counting," said Viridienne. "Limited numbers drive a market as well, but I think buying one and then locking it up really stinks. But that's not where I'm going with my research. I can tell you more when I come down there and we can talk face-to-face. I really appreciate this. Thank you."

"Tell me, why did you choose Nicolo Brandosi as one of your ten?"

Viridienne spoke carefully. "Mostly for personal reasons. He's local—I mean, New England. That's being a little offhand, I guess. Sorry. The point is, I think his work is amazing. I mean, it encompasses so much. It's of its time, but it's also timeless in its depth and design. At least, that's how I see it. That's really the common denominator in the artists I've chosen. Maybe I can explain it this way. Take Andrew Wyeth…"

"I wish I could. Maybe just three or four." Van Daam gave a modest chuckle.

"No, really. There's lots of people who can render something as well as he can, but I believe his timeless genius comes from the fact that even when he paints an empty room, you feel like you know the person who's just walked out of there. And the designs of his paintings are every bit as elegant as the images themselves. Everything comes together. That's what I'm looking for."

"You're really into this, aren't you?"

Viridienne smiled and nodded even though the woman on the other end of the call couldn't see her.

"Do you make art yourself, or do you just study and write about it? You seem to be very knowledgeable about what goes into making a piece of art as well as what makes people want to buy it."

"I'm a fiber artist." She laughed. "Possibly the least understood and collected art in the western and eastern hemispheres put together. My research has done me absolutely no good as far as my own sales are concerned. Like most artists, I work so I can support my habit."

"Sorry to interrupt, but someone's just come in to the gallery. I have to go. But why don't you email me a couple of pictures of your work, and if they're not too cumbersome, bring one or two with you when you come in? I'd like to see what you are doing."

"Wow," said Viridienne. "Sure."

Viridienne had only just ended the call when the phone pinged, announcing that she had a message. She looked at the ID and saw that it was a text from Yanni.

"Funeral Wednesday next week, 11 a.m. We meet at the funeral home at 9. Family gathering afterward. You can stay at the house if it gets late. Details to follow. TTYL."

Chapter Forty-Four

On that same Monday morning, Detectives Grey and Fitzpatrick were comparing notes over midmorning coffee.

"I understand the body's going to be released to the family later today," said Fitzpatrick. "I'd like to know what plans they've made for the funeral. I mean, it's not like I can just give them a call and ask."

"Actually, I think you probably could, but it might be better to call Viridienne. I'll bet you anything she'll know, and if she doesn't, I'm sure she'll appreciate the information. I suspect she'll want to go." Grey gave him a sideways look. "You could look at the obituaries."

"I did. Nada. A minimal announcement of the death, followed by 'Arrangements incomplete.' Not much to go on there. Didn't even list a funeral home."

"This whole thing is weird."

He toasted her with his coffee container. "Tell me about it."

"I know the forensic team has been all over the house and yard. Anything significant there?"

He shook his head. "Not a thing. The murderer knew his stuff. Not a fingerprint on anything. No shoe impressions in the snow, nothing under the fingernails, nothing dropped or ripped off... nothing. Clean sweep."

"So where are we on the case itself?"

"Not very far. She died from a single blow to the back of the head. Pretty much instantaneous. Whoever it was knew their business." He grimaced. "There was no sign of forced entry. That means she likely knew her killer and let him in. So we start checking friends, family, and associates."

She nodded. "And from what Viridienne told us, and what her family told us, they've had virtually no contact for the last ten years. As far as I'm concerned, family is probably a nonissue."

He shook his head. "Uh-uh. Her family, maybe, but not the Brandosis. Someone from that side had to come up every so often and collect the latest cache of newly discovered paintings."

"Agreed, but like I said before, it makes no sense to kill the goose that lays—or in her case, paints—the golden eggs. That piece doesn't add up. Still, I suppose it's a starting point."

"It's a long shot," said Fitz, "but I haven't counted out professional jealousy or a rejected lover somewhere."

She looked puzzled. "Professional jealousy? You thinking maybe someone from the Mayflower group? Someone who carried a secret passion for her, got rejected, and went crazy?"

"Not really," said Fitz, pulling on his chin with his thumb. "But right now, anything's possible. I'd hate to miss something right under my nose because I made a false assumption."

"So it's back to the gallery?"

"I think we go back to the house first and, from there, on to the gallery. It might make sense to bring Viridienne along with us when we go."

Allison cocked a curious eye at her partner. "Fitzy ditzy witzy boy, if I didn't know better, I would start to begin to think that maybe you are looking for reasons to involve the overly tall and slender older-than-you Viridienne Greene in our operation. Like, what's going on, dude?" She leaned over and smacked him on the shoulder. "Not professional, dude. Boundaries, dude."

Fitz tried really hard not to blush, but his fair Irish skin would not play along. His cheeks burned, and he looked up and stared at the ceiling.

"Jesus, Fitz! Well, this is a first. Never thought I'd see the day. I had you pegged for a future priest, for God's sake."

"Hardly." He chuckled self-consciously. "I am a professional. I drank the Kool-Aid. I took the oath, and I value and respect the job I do. I have never and will never mix my personal life with my professional life."

"Okay, so what about after the case is closed?"

"Then the case is closed."

She fixed him with a steady eye. "Fitz, do you think you should take yourself off the case?"

"No, Alison, I don't. If there's one thing the Irish know

how to do better than anyone else, it's keeping secrets. We simply don't talk about anything personal."

"I want to believe you, Detective Fitzpatrick."

"You have every reason to believe me, Detective Grey."

She flashed him a thumbs-up. "Okay, then, let's get on with it. Why don't I call Ms. Greene and set up a time to go back into the house before the family lays claim to it? Hopefully she's available today. The sooner the better."

He nodded. "You finished with your coffee?" He held out his hand for her cup. "I'll toss these and go see what else is on the docket. It's not like this is the only thing we're working on."

"It's the nastiest, though, and I have the distinct feeling that it's going to be downhill all the way from here."

He responded with a grim nod, dropped the two empty containers in the wastebasket beside the desk, and headed out into the corridor.

"Proceed with caution, Detective," whispered Alison into the empty office.

Chapter Forty-Five

Early that same afternoon, Fitzpatrick, Alison, and Viridienne pulled up almost simultaneously in front of Rose Doré's silent, empty house. The air outside was cold but not biting, and the persistent wind off the harbor had decided to take the afternoon off. If their business had not been so grim, it might have been a good day for a winter walk followed by a cup of hot chocolate with lots of whipped cream.

Viridienne had her key out and in hand by the time they were on the front porch. She leaned forward to unlock the door then stopped midturn.

"I... uh... damn!" She shook her head. "I didn't think it was going to be this hard."

"Do you want me to go in first?" asked Fitz. "I can go in and turn on some lights, and you can stay here with Alison until you're ready to come in.

Viridienne shook her head, emphatically, "No. Thank you anyway, but I need to do this. I need to be the first one to come back in here. A friend, not a stranger." And with more force than was necessary, she twisted the key in the lock and pushed hard to open the door.

When she couldn't do it, Fitz stepped up and used his square, sturdy self as a battering ram. "Jaysus, Mary, and Joseph," gasped Fitz, jumping back and out of the way.

"Oh my God," said Viridienne.

"Holy shit," said Alison, a woman not given to four-letter words.

The three were greeted by a low wave of ice-cold water gushing out of the door, over their feet, across the front porch, and down onto the snow-covered front lawn. When the worst of it was out, the three waded in, not knowing what to expect… and not a one of them could have been prepared for that they found. The house had been totally ransacked. Whoever had gotten into the place had torn it up and viciously destroyed everything within reach. Furniture was slashed, dishes and glassware were smashed, and every faucet in the place had been opened and left running into plugged-up sinks.

"The paintings," yelled Viridienne, sloshing through the ice-cold water toward the stairs.

Futile as it was, Fitz ran around the house, shutting off the faucets, while Alison and Viridienne splashed upstairs to Rose's studio… where the damage was even worse. Tubes of paint were crushed and exploded all over the floor. Brushes were broken in half and rolls of canvas slashed, and gesso—that quick-drying cover-all paint artists use to prime a canvas—had been poured over everything. And in all of the devastation, there was not a painting, not even a half-finished one, anywhere.

"Jaysus," said Fitz, as he sloshed into the studio. "This is just plain vicious."

"She kept her own paintings locked up in the attic," said Viridienne, her voice and everything else about her shaking. "I don't have a key, but I'm sure we can break in. I saw you take on the front door. You can't make anything any worse than it already is." She paused, looking at the devastation surrounding them. "Who in the world would do such thing?"

Fitz and Alison answered as one. "The killer... and he was very angry."

"I think we've got ourselves a real nutjob here," said Alison. "As if killing the poor woman wasn't enough, he had to trash everything she owned as well."

"And we both know that nutjobs don't usually stop once they've tasted blood." Fitzpatrick stepped carefully through the mess on the floor and walked toward the landing outside the room. "Let's see what's left in the attic."

"Let's see what's left *of* the attic," rejoined Alison.

The answer, when they opened the unlocked door, was... nothing. Well, almost nothing. The smell was over-powering. The attic had been emptied of everything inorganic, but in the empty space was a large fecal calling card obscenely ornamented with paintbrushes dipped in Alizarin crimson.

Viridienne gasped and turned away. Alison made a face and covered her mouth and nose. "Well, I'd say there's no question that the same person who killed Rose Doré came back and did his best to wipe out everything she owned or ever touched. That's some calling card."

Fitz herded the two women back out of the room and down the stairs ahead of him. When they were on the first floor, all of them shaking with cold because of their wet feet and the chill in the house, he was the first to speak. "This just got even worse than it already was. I believe we are dealing with a psychopath, and one who might not think he's finished with obliterating every trace of Rose Doré and desecrating her memory. We got one sick puppy on our hands—a sick and dangerous puppy. The mentally ill are the worst. They are not bad people—they're sick. When you have a cold or even pneumonia, your brain might be fuzzy, but it's still intact. The mentally ill will often go by the rules that are inside their own heads and construct a reality in which their actions are perfectly reasonable and justified."

"To them," added Alison.

"What are you saying?" asked Viridienne.

"I'm saying that you, as Rose's best and only friend—someone who had a key to her house and knew where she kept her own paintings and who she was doing the other paintings for—you could very possibly become a target for this man's obsession as well."

Viridienne shivered.

"Clearly, whoever killed her knew her habits. Knew her schedule. Watched her… saw her with you on more than one occasion, right?"

"Probably." Viridienne was now shaking all over.

"You're freezing, and so are we. We need to get out of here and get you some dry shoes and socks. But I don't want you going back to your house tonight."

"What are you talking about? I can't leave my cat

alone… and now that I think of it, I don't want to leave my house alone, either."

"Why don't you come back to the station with us before you make a decision? We can stop at a Target or a Walmart for some shoes and socks. My treat. Then, once we are warmed up and dried off, we can think about what to do about you and your safety and about the house and the mess we're standing in."

"I would think it's the Stamos family who will have final say over what happens to the house now," said Alison. "I'll make the call to Yanni and tell him what's happened. Good God, as if they don't have enough to deal with. Now this."

"You can do that when we get back to the station. Dry feet first." He paused and turned toward Viridienne. "Do you mind if Alison rides in your car with you? You've had a rough day, and God only knows whether or not you can still feel your feet. But I'd feel better if she went with you. I'll go secure the place, then I'll drive your car back."

Viridienne wasn't used to being looked after. It was weird. But the detective was right. She was freezing and she wasn't thinking clearly… and in two days' time, she'd be going, as a member of the family, to Rose's funeral.

WHEN THE TWO WOMEN WERE SAFELY OUT OF SIGHT, Fitz returned to the demolished house and once again climbed the stairs to the attic. In the doorway, he pulled his scarf over his mouth and nose and an evidence bag out of his pocket. After pulling on a pair of rubber gloves and further shielding his hands with the evidence bag, he picked up the disgusting pile, knotted it off and dropped it into a second bag. "Bingo!"

The sicko who had done this could not have realized that what he left was far superior to fingerprints, hairs, or skin scrapings. This was as valuable as his social security card and his driver's license. *Fresh DNA.* And unlike a license or a social security card, it could not be faked. He would deliver it straight to Forensics.

Detective Fitzpatrick was a happy man.

Chapter Forty-Six

In less than an hour, Alison and Viridienne were seated in Fitz's office with warm, dry feet, holding oversized cups of hot chocolate with double whipped cream. Fitz guessed that the combination of chocolate and warm feet would be almost—but not quite—delicious enough to take away the sting of why they were sitting there in the first place. Alison was asking the questions this time, and Fitz was taking notes.

Viridienne rubbed her eyes with her free hand. "I still can't get my head around the fact that killing her wasn't enough. Even stealing the paintings makes some kind of sick sense to me. But why did whoever it was come back and destroy her house on top of that?"

"Someone was intent on obliterating every trace of her," said Fitz, scribbling on the pad in front of him. "But I can't get ahead of myself. I need more facts."

"Oh my God."

"What's the matter, Viridienne?" asked Fitz.

"The house. The mess. We've got to tell the family what's happened so they can get someone to clean it up. Everything is going to rot and freeze in there."

Fitz held up a restraining hand. "Much as I hate to, I'm going to wait on that until after the forensics team has gone through it. It's still a crime scene and off limits to everyone. By the look of it, I'd say it's a total loss, and a day or two isn't going to make any difference one way or the other in the wreckage or the restoration. They'll be lucky if they can even save the structure. Beautiful old house, though. Shame to see it like that."

Alison cleared her throat and changed the subject. "We got word from the medical examiner that they've released the body. Do we know when the funeral will be?"

Viridienne rolled her eyes. "Good grief. My mind is turning into Jell-O. I forgot to tell you, Yanni called and asked me to have coffee with him the other day. He wanted to talk about his sister… you know, what I knew about her life in Plymouth."

Fitz and Alison both sat at attention.

"When was this?" asked Fitz, his voice tight.

"The day after we went to Providence to see the Stamos family."

"But if the body hadn't been released, how could he know about when the funeral would be?"

"He didn't at first. He called me again last night and said I've been invited to sit with the family. I guess it's an honor, but I'm still in a fog. I don't think any of this has really registered yet."

Fitz and Alison went over the existing facts one more time and learned absolutely nothing new. Everything Viridienne said checked out with everything she'd said before. With no new questions, there was no reason to keep asking the old ones over again. Expressing their genuine condolences, they thanked her for coming. They reminded her to lock her doors, not to talk to strangers or anyone from the media, and to be in touch if anything aroused her suspicions then sent her on her way in her new dry shoes.

When she was well out of earshot, Fitz turned to his partner. "Looks like we are going back to the Mayflower Gallery to do some more digging around."

"And making another *condolence* call on brother Yanni. We already know there's a mob involvement here, and I'm sure her brother knows something—if not everything—about the 'discovered' Brandosi paintings. Remember, according to Viridienne, who was told by Rose, the two families made a bargain with the devil: silence, a newly relocated all-expenses-paid life, and the continued safety of her family in exchange for a steady stream of paintings, no questions asked."

Alison was looking darkly troubled. "You're looking at some seriously dangerous stuff here, my friend."

"No kidding, Alison, but what other choice do I have?"

"What choice do *we* have, partner?"

"Nada. I'll call Providence PD and set up an info meeting. I'll try to coordinate it with the next visit with the Stamos family later in the week. Might as well let them get the funeral out of the way first before we mess up another day for them."

"You want me to call the gallery?"

Fitz shook his head. "No. I think I'd just like to drop in by myself and surprise them. I seriously don't think there's any criminal involvement there, but someone might have noticed something or recorded some phone calls or overheard a conversation. Remember, someone was watching her."

"More like stalking her... and whoever it is, he's still out there, and he's getting more desperate."

"So what are you telling me? You still following the professional-jealousy thread or the rejected-lover theory?"

Alison chewed on her lip. "Right now, nothing's off the table. You know that. The thing is, killing Rose wasn't enough. After that, whoever it was totally wrecked the house and took all the paintings. Who is going to be next?"

"Do you think Viridienne's on the list? And if so, should we have let her go home? Maybe we should put a detail on her and the house. I'd hate to have her become collateral damage."

"I'd be lying if I said I hadn't already thought of it," said Alison, "but let's see what we can find out at the gallery, what Yanni has to say, and what the forensic team turns up at the house before I put a formal detail on her. Meanwhile, what I will do is have the guys on the street do some extra drive-bys and keep an eye on the place."

"Too bad she lives so far out."

"Tell me about it. When do you plan to go over to the gallery?" Alison asked.

"Tomorrow afternoon after the daily briefing?"

"That works. If that's it for the day, then I'm going to pack up and head home. I need to do a little grocery shopping. The natives in the Grey household are getting restless."

Detective Fitzpatrick checked his cell phone and was

gratified to see a short text, "TKU," and a smiley face. He had not bothered to tell his colleague he'd texted his private phone number to Viridienne, asking her to keep it on speed dial in case of an emergency or in case anything came to mind that she thought might be of help to the investigation. No harm in that.

Lost in the winds of remembering
I see the carefree days
The little boy skipping stones with his da
Trying so hard to best him
Always my three to his five
Trying so hard to best him
Until the day I did.

Chapter Forty-Seven

O bedient Thankful was sitting at the kitchen table with Cam and Donna and the four kids, discussing her new name. Needless to say, each of the kids, even the boys, wanted her to pick one of their names. In amongst elbows, glasses of milk, and a plate of cookies were five pieces of paper with the final considerations. In no particular order, they were: Emily Rose, Dorothy Jean, Elizabeth Anne, and Jeanne Marie. She had already asked if she could take their family name, Spencer, as her surname.

One by one, amidst the happy chatter, names were eliminated until only two remained on the table, Emily Rose and Elizabeth Anne. The family members would vote, and Thankful would abstain. She was content to let her new family choose her new forever name. The winning name was Emily Rose. *Emily Rose Spencer. Game on!*

Chapter Forty-Eight

L ate morning on Tuesday, almost a week after the murder, the mood inside the Mayflower Gallery and artisan gift shop was restrained. Tourists visiting from elsewhere wouldn't have noticed anything, but the artists, the volunteers, and even some curious townspeople were subdued in both speech and action. Absent was the customary cheery, gossipy banter and the enthusiastic welcome extended to all and sundry who came through the door. Despite the efficiency of the central heating, an uncomfortable, unmentionable chill hung in the air and collected in the corners.

The midwinter exhibit would remain in place until the end of February. Out of respect for Rose, the spaces where her paintings had originally been hung were left empty. In mute testimony to what had happened, only a small white card bearing the title of the absent piece and the artist's name was left on display.

Even though he wasn't on the schedule, Jackson Smith

had come in every day since they'd received the news of Rose's death. He was totally at loose ends since it had happened—coming in, puttering around, and looking for things to do and fix and clean must have given him a sense of purpose. At least, that was what the board members surmised, and out of sympathy for his evident distress, they found any number of little tasks to keep him busy.

PAULINE DELAAR WAS AT THE DESK WHEN DETECTIVE Fitzpatrick walked through the front door. She smiled an uncomfortable smile—all teeth and no eyes. "Well, hello again, Detective. What brings you in today? Are you here on duty or to see the show?"

He favored her with smile and a raised an index-finger half salute. "Duty, I'm afraid, but I might as well take a look at the show as long as I'm here."

"If it's duty, please let me know if there's anything I or one of the volunteers can do to be of help."

"Thank you, ma'am. Actually, if you don't mind, I'd like to ask you and some of the volunteers a couple of questions."

"If it's about Rose…"

He held up his hand. "Not about Rose—not directly, anyway. Do you sit at the desk most days?"

She sat up a little straighter. "I do. I am the president of the association, and sitting at the desk gives me a way to watch and be useful at the same time. You know, greeting people, keeping an eye on loose kids, telling people where to find the bathroom, even answering tourist questions…

being the public face of the association." She gave him a real smile this time.

"Thank you, ma'am. And you answer the phone?"

She nodded. "I always check the ID first, and sometimes, I confess, I let the machine answer it."

"Can you tell me if you remember any unusual phone calls or any callers who might have asked about Rose or her teaching or her artwork?"

She made a thinking face. "Nothing that really stands out. I mean, people were calling all the time, asking about her classes. She was a very popular instructor. Especially with the kids. They just loved her." She gave a long sigh then added in a much softer tone, "We all did. She was… something else."

"How so?

"Wait a minute. Now that you mention it, I do remember something. It wasn't a phone call, though—it was one of the visitors."

Fitz held his breath. "What was that, ma'am?"

"Every so often over the last year, a man would come in here and walk slowly around the gallery. He looked at everything, I mean, really looked. Stopped and looked. So many people just walk around here with a glazed look, in and out in five minutes. He would stay at least an hour, looking at every single piece. Sometimes, he even took photographs and made notes. I remember asking him if he was from a TV station or the local paper."

"What did he say?"

"He said he was just an art lover, and coming into the gallery was like spending time with old friends. He seemed lonely. I never saw him come in here with anyone."

"So he was a regular visitor."

She paused. "Hmmm... I guess he was. Not all that regular. I mean, not like every week, but regular enough that we had a passing acquaintance. Came in a couple or three times a year."

"Did he tell you his name?"

"You know what? He never did... but then, I never asked either. I guess that makes us even."

"Can you remember what he looked like?"

She nodded. "Kinda made me wish I was about twenty years younger. He wasn't very tall. I mean, like, average or maybe a little shorter. Not fat but not skinny. Kind of olive-colored skin, dark eyes... and *gorgeous* hair. Dark and wavy, every strand in place." She held a conspiratorial hand to the side of her mouth. "He probably sprayed it." Then she pointed to her own short-cropped white hair. "I'd kill for that hair... if you get my drift."

"Hi, Pauline... good grief, Fitz. What are you doing here?" Accompanied by a blast of cold air and the crash of the front door slamming shut behind her, Viridienne Greene, her signature cape swirling around her, had exploded into the gallery and immediately expanded to fill any remaining space.

With his back to Pauline, Fitz shot her a warning glance and crossed his two hands, palms out, in the universal *say nothing* signal.

"You two know each other?" asked Pauline.

"Viridienne made the 911 call the night Rose was killed," said Fitz. "Let's just say we met under very difficult circumstances.

Pauline nodded in the very picture of sympathetic

understanding. "Well, let's hope you two can get on better footing when this awfulness is over and done with. Um, I hope you don't mind if I ask you, Detective, but how's the search for the... uh...?"

"Killer?" he supplied. "*In progress* is the best answer I can give. It's not something we can talk about when the case is active."

"Of course. It was foolish of me to ask." She started fussing with the papers on the desk in front of her.

"No, it would be foolish if I answered it," he responded. "But you couldn't know that. No harm done." He smiled. "Now, on a much more attractive subject, Ms. Greene, since you are right here and I don't know much about art—but I do know what I like—I wonder if you'd take me around to see your work." He gave her a conspiratorial wink.

Viridienne never missed a beat. "Right this way, Detective. I'm what's called a fiber artist. I make art out of pieces of string that are too short to use and too good to throw out."

When the two were well away from the busy lady on the front desk, Viridienne tapped Fitzpatrick on the arm and whispered, "You know I'll be going to the funeral day after tomorrow."

He paused for a fraction of a second before responding in a whisper of his own. "I hate to ask you this, and it's totally out of police protocol, but I wonder if you could be my eyes and ears when you go. You're going to be sitting with the family, and that puts you in a perfect position to hear anything and everything they say. You might just pick up something useful."

Viridienne chewed on her lip and looked away from Fitzpatrick's Irish blue eyes then nodded. "I can do that for you."

AFTER FITZPATRICK LEFT THE GALLERY, A SUBDUED AND thoughtful Viridienne went back into the office. *Life is supposed to go on,* she told herself as she checked on her class numbers for the upcoming session. The sooner she got herself back into her own predictable routine, the better it would be. But as she flipped through the file folders, she came across the one belonging to Rose, and it all came back.

She carried it out to give to Pauline. "I just found this. We should probably get rid of it along with her teaching stuff."

Pauline held out her hand. "I suppose, but I can't just throw it all out. Tell you what—I'll gather up anything that's personal and put it in a box. Then if there is a next of kin anywhere, we can give it to them."

Viridienne hesitated and continued to hold on to the folder. "Tell *you* what—why don't I do that right now? I'll collect her personal things. I'll check in her classroom too. She had a stash of stuff in there. I'll get it all together, show it to you so you know what I've got, and then box it up."

"I wonder if it's something that detective might want. You know, evidence or such?"

"Good point," said Viridienne. "One never knows."

"And speaking of 'one never knows,' have you seen or

talked to Jackson Smith lately? He's taking this Rose thing very badly."

"What do you mean?"

Pauline did enjoy a bit of gossip. She leaned forward on her elbows to deliver it sotto voce. "He's very agitated and spacey, and he's repeating himself even more than usual. He tried to empty the trash three times in one hour. Kept forgetting he'd already done it. Then he couldn't find his car keys… he was like a wild man looking for them. Kept saying one of the gallery visitors must have taken them and then running outside to see if his car was still there."

"Did he finally find them?"

Pauline nodded. "He left them in his jacket, different pocket. He always puts them in his pants pocket. Then he was all apologies for causing such a fuss. He drove us all nuts. I told him to go home and pull himself together. In a kind way, of course. He always means well, but we all know how he can get when something upsets him."

Viridienne rolled her eyes. "Tell me about it. And you're right—he always means well. He's just fragile. Oh yeah, and by the way, I'll be going to the funeral."

"I thought the arrangements were private."

"They are," said Viridienne.

Chapter Forty-Nine

In Greek tradition, much as in Jewish tradition, it was the custom to have the visitation and the funeral as soon as possible after the day of death. That the funeral took place almost a full week after the event—it was so hard to say the word *murder*—only added to everyone's distress. But Yanni—the man in charge, the youngest son, and the one who heretofore had performed the fewest of the family duties and carried the least of the family responsibilities—was taking care of everything.

He was doing his best to keep a clear head and maintain some sort of balance. Grief, anger, and vengefulness warred with each other in his brain and in his heart. He would deal with each of these emotions in due time. For the moment, he concerned himself with funeral arrangements—*final arrangements*—for his only baby sister.

The funeral itself would be held at the Church of the Annunciation in the neighboring city of Attleboro, Massachusetts. There would be no visitation hours before the funeral, no vigil—only the funeral itself with Xenia dressed in white and lying in an open casket. According to custom, it would be facing east, and at the proper time, people could file past and bless her with a final *kiss of peace.*

VIRIDIENNE HAD BEEN IN VERY FEW CHURCHES SINCE beginning life on the outside. She'd left all thoughts of God, organized religion, and church buildings behind her the night she escaped the compound. And if the guest of honor had not been her friend Rose, she would not have come to this one either.

As she drove south on the back roads, following the directions her cell phone bleated at her, she felt like a mechanical doll with someone else pulling the strings. The reality of where she was going and why she was going there had finally established itself in her mind. Rose was dead, and she was going to say her last goodbye before learning to live without her friend.

She fiercely blinked away the unbidden tears so she could see the road ahead and wondered how long it would take before the spontaneous fits of weeping would stop. But that thought was interrupted by the uncomfortable reality that because she was not a regular churchgoer—much less a Greek Orthodox churchgoer—she had no idea how to conduct herself. Fortunately, Yanni, in declaring her family, had insisted that she meet them all at the funeral home for a private viewing then ride with him in one of the family cars in the cortege.

Out of respect for the family, she had taken care to set

aside her signature flamboyant colorful artsy skirts and flowing scarves and instead was wearing loose black slacks, a long black tunic sweater, and a single strand of silver beads. She kept her silver hoop earrings, and with no black funeral coat to wear, she chose a thick dark-purple shawl she'd woven some years before. The effect was dramatic but decorous.

Yanni met her in the parking lot and personally directed her to an empty space at the back, where, he explained, the car would be safe until she was ready to leave. She thanked him, gave him a quick hug, and followed him to the entrance, where a group of black-clad men and women were speaking quietly on the outside steps. He took her elbow and steered her through the mourners and into the dimly lighted interior of the funeral home itself. This was uncharted territory for Viridienne, and she was grateful for Yanni's reassuring presence. Without a word, he led her into a room and to an open bronze casket surrounded by banks of flowers. Viridienne squeezed her eyes shut and turned away.

Yanni took her hand and gave it a reassuring squeeze. "No, Viridienne, don't look away. She looks beautiful. Peaceful. I want you to remember her this way… not the other way."

Viridienne opened her eyes and looked down at her friend. Yanni was right. If she had to remember her, she wanted it to be like this, not crumpled on the floor of her studio. Rose was finally at peace, and so was Xenia. She took a deep breath, stepped forward, leaned over the body of her friend, and kissed her cold forehead. Then she took a scrap of yarn out of her pocket, tucked it into one of the folds of the white dress, and whispered a last goodbye.

"I was going to knit her a scarf," she said softly. "This was the yarn she'd picked out." Viridienne turned to Yanni and sniffed and smiled. "You know what she was like—an absolute perfectionist, right down to the colors she painted with and she wore."

Yanni chuckled as he led Viridienne out of the room and toward where the funeral cars were lining up.

"We all called her a control freak. *Perfectionist* sounds a little nicer."

"She was my friend. We understood each other."

Yanni leaned in and whispered, "Come with me. You are sitting with us in the first car. When we get to the church, just stay next to me, and I'll show you what to do."

The funeral service was like nothing she had ever experienced. From the moment she walked in with the family, following the casket, into the most ornate interior she'd ever seen, she felt a sense of overwhelming peace. She couldn't name it, nor at the moment would she try, but maybe one day, she would return and try to understand what had happened. Her head and her heart were filled with echoing sounds of the ethereal, haunting music, the stylized paintings and mosaics that covered every inch of the space, and the curious, vaguely familiar smell of incense. Somehow, it had all come together in a moving and fitting tribute to her friend. Her beloved Rose had finally come home.

At the conclusion, the funeral director led the quiet procession out of the church and stood to one side as the casket was lifted into the hearse. They all knew the burial would be sometime in the spring. They stood, in cold, silent tribute as the boxy black vehicle drove out of sight.

Viridienne was experiencing total emotional and visual overload. The raucous family—now laughing and crying all at the same time—the prayers and anthems in a language she couldn't understand... and the curious comfort and discomfort she felt sitting close to Yanni—all of that and more, she would sort out later in the privacy of her own home. Meanwhile, there was a lot more of the day to get through. She turned her thoughts to the upcoming meal and realized she was starving. She'd been too upset to eat anything before she left the house. Her empty stomach was letting her—and everyone in earshot—know that it had had enough of this privation.

Yanni grinned and nudged her with his elbow. "Won't be long now, sister. I'm hungry too."

Chapter Fifty

A cross the street from the church, in an upscale coffee shop, the man was leaning on his elbows over an ice-cold cup of coffee. He watched, stone-faced, as the line of family cars pulled away from the curb one by one. He, too, had to go home and do some thinking. If Viridienne Greene was riding in the family car next to the one man in the Stamos family who could spell trouble for everyone, he needed to get moving.

He left the untouched coffee on the table, dropped a five-dollar bill beside it, and left without pushing in his chair. Instead of getting easier, this whole thing was getting more complicated by the minute. If Viridienne was sitting in the bosom of the family, the man was dead certain that she knew everything. He didn't like being in the killing business, but Rose had left him no choice.

Chapter Fifty-One

Obedient Thankful was a thing of the past. In her place was Emily Rose Spencer. The name change was now official, and she even had her own social security number to go with it. It took some time and some digging to find her birth records, but when the Spencers explained that she'd been born into the Society of Obedient Believers, the people in the records department knew exactly where to look.

She'd been making steady progress and was pleased to discover that she had a real aptitude for numbers and, more specifically, computers. Her secret hours spent at the computer in the compound office had paid off, and it wasn't long before she had a job in the financial office of a local utility company, a bike she could ride to work, and a driver's learning permit. The one thing she didn't have was her sister, and in truth, she was conflicted about starting the search.

It was Donna who finally set things in motion. One

night after supper, they were drying dishes and chatting about their respective days. Donna had a small catering business and worked from home, and Emily was chatting easily about work and her colleagues—a normal, everyday, unrestricted conversation between two women who enjoyed each other's company. Donna seized on the convivial moment and asked how and when she was going to start looking for her sister and whether she needed any help.

Emily went silent for a few minutes. Then she looked up at Donna. "I want to more than anything, and I'm totally scared to do it. What if she's forgotten me? Maybe she doesn't want a kid sister showing up in the middle of her life. What if she's married and has kids and has no room for me?"

Donna folded her dish towel over the edge of the sink and held up both hands. "Whoa, girl. That's called ambivalence... and it's natural enough. But there's only one way to find out. Go get your laptop. We'll do it together."

Chapter Fifty-Two

E ven though Yanni made it abundantly clear that Viridienne was more than welcome to stay the night with them all in the family home, she declined. She did accept the invitation to go back to the house after the *Makaria*—the funeral meal—as much to rest up from all that eating as anything else. She was so full that she had to unbutton her slacks. Viridienne was a healthy eater, but even she had reached her limit and was looking forward to some quiet time and maybe a cup of coffee with Yanni and the rest of the family before heading home.

But when she entered the house, looking only for a chair to collapse into, she discovered that another whole spread had been laid out on the dining room table for the immediate family. And despite her abdominal distress and distension, her heart and her mind were comforted by the lavish excess. *This is love made visible—and edible*, she thought and graciously accepted a small cup of thick bitter black coffee and a tiny square of baklava.

Later, as she was walking out the door, Yanni caught her arm and wrapped her in a firm full-body hug. His head came up to her nose. "Thank you so much for being here today, Viridienne. We all know how hard this must have been for you, and we all really appreciate it. I can only hope you'll come back and join us for the Easter service. It's really something to experience. And afterward, you can see everyone, and the food will be even better."

Food was the last thing on Viridienne's mind by then. She was sure she wouldn't eat for a week. "Thank you for making me feel so welcome, Yanni. This whole thing is terrible, and I guess we've all done the best we can."

Yanni stepped back, his hands still resting on her shoulders, and looked up at her. "Be careful, little big sister." They both smiled. "Listen, I'm serious about keeping your head down. These people don't fool around. They shoot first and ask questions afterward. I'm going to find out who killed my sister. When I do, I'll let you know the case is closed."

"You're not going to tell me who?"

"Not on your life, lady, not on your life. Drive safely, and shoot me a text when you get home, okay?"

"Okay."

They stood looking at one another for a moment, an arm's length apart on the porch of the big old house. Then Yanni stepped forward, rose up on his toes, and kissed her. "One for the road… and don't forget to text me."

Yanni remained on the front porch until Viridienne's car was out of sight, then he turned back into the house and went directly into the kitchen. The after-after meal had been catered, so the staff had done the major part of the clearing away, but the house wasn't completely back to normal. Yanni liked keeping things the way they were supposed to be and putting things back where they belonged. He actually enjoyed wiping down the counters in the kitchen. It was calming and restorative after such a heart-twisting bitch of a day. The mindless busy-work of cleaning up also helped him think.

There was no question in his mind that someone directly or indirectly connected to the Brandosi family had killed his sister. When it was a family-against-family vendetta, it didn't really matter who'd actually done the deed… but actually, it did matter. He gave the sodden dish-cloth he was holding a savage twist.

He was wading into very dark waters, and he knew it. On the one hand, he could drop a few helpful words and names on the anonymous tip line and leave it to the police to catch the murderer. The idea had merit and would likely not endanger his family any further. On the other hand, Yanni had wanted to see that bastard Brandosi bleed ever since he'd first raised a hand to his sister. Then someone had robbed him of the pleasure and done a perfect job of making it look like an accident—another nameless, twisted alley of dark secrets and family grudges wherein everyone knew the real story and, in silent accord, agreed to bury it because to do otherwise would have resulted in more bloodshed. But the Brandosis had been left with the upper hand, which Yanni and the brothers Stamos would not forget. It was a waiting game. The cobra was in the basket for the moment, but the day would come when Yanni would tip over that basket and turn the snake loose.

Chapter Fifty-Three

Viridienne thought about the quick kiss that Yanni had left on her cheek and quickly dismissed it as an act of brotherly affection and concern. Men getting too close, uninvited, still scared the bejesus out of her. *Concentrate on your driving, Viridienne.*

The night was beautifully moonlit. But the brilliant-white light cast long dark tree shadows across fields of pristine snow and would, without warning, plunge her into an instant blackout on the twisting back road that was taking her home. Keeping her focus on the road was easier said than done. Her artist's mind was flashing back to the colors, sounds, images, and smells inside the Greek Orthodox cathedral. If she ever went to church again, she would want it to be one like that. Her stomach was reminding her that she'd eaten way too much, but that, too, was a pleasant memory, even if the seat belt did feel a bit constraining.

Her grieving mind was still saying goodbye to her friend. Her dutiful mind remembered to tell her to text Fitzpatrick when she got back to the house... and her preoccupied mind only vaguely registered the car that had been following her ever since she'd left the Stamos house.

Chapter Fifty-Four

"So if we are going to start looking for your sister, let's begin with Facebook," said Donna. "You on Facebook yet?"

Emily looked down at her hands, which were folded in her lap. "I don't have any friends yet, so no, I'm not on Facebook. It didn't make any sense."

"No matter—I am. And we're going to do a Google search too."

"Um, what's a Google search?"

"Haven't you done that sort of thing at work? You know, look up something on Google."

Emily said, "Yes, but it's always work related. I've never done it for myself. I haven't even shopped online yet."

Donna wrapped a motherly arm around the young woman standing next to her. "Well, I have. Let's get going. You fire up your laptop, and I'll go get mine."

Emily was still looking doubtful.

"We are just looking. You know how when you go into

a store, you look around before you actually buy anything?"

Emily nodded.

"Well, it's the same thing. First, we're going to look around and see what's out there. Then, if we do find something that looks promising, we can decide whether or not to keep on going. Even if we actually find her, or the person who is most likely her, you can still decide whether or not to contact her. See what I mean?"

"But what if someone at the society sees it?" said Emily. "What if they send someone out after me?

"Got that covered too. First of all, you're of legal age. They can't make you do anything. Now, in the beginning, we open an anonymous Hotmail or Yahoo account using any name you want. It's free, and it's a safety precaution against scammers and spammers. When you feel more comfortable using all of this, you can open an account in your own brand-new name."

Emily covered her eyes with both hands. "I am so stupid. I have a new name, and the elders have no idea what it is. I can use my own name if I want to."

"That's my girl." Donna raised a warning finger. "But let's save that nice new name for when we really need it."

Chapter Fifty-Five

The house was dark and cold when Viridienne dragged herself through the door—dark, cold, and blessedly familiar. She flicked on the lights. *Home.* The soft hum of the various appliances was comforting and familiar. Even the feel of DT rubbing her ankles, reminding her it was well past his suppertime, was comforting.

She tossed her outer clothing onto the nearest available surface, pushed up the thermostat, and headed for the cat-food department. Food was the last thing on her mind, but there was no need to deprive her furry housemate of his dinner.

After the cat was fed and her sofa bed pulled out and set up, she dropped into her chair and pulled out her knitting. Too wound up from the day's events to fall asleep immediately, she decided that knitting and a full glass of wine—for medicinal purposes, of course—would eventually relax her and summon the gods and goddesses of sleep. No TV, no music, no NPR... just quiet.

She was slipping into a meditative doze when the sound of a branch snapping somewhere out front brought her back into the moment. *A deer*, she told herself. Their tracks were all over the snow. Poor things were looking everywhere for food.

Tomorrow, I'll call the gallery in New York and set up an appointment... and yes, I will bring a couple of my own pieces with me. She decided that after that, she might just take a quick drive down to Providence and look into Gallery 57. She'd give no advance phone call but just wander in, introduce herself as Valerie Stone, and see what happened.

Her cell phone rudely interrupted that particular little mental meander. It was Yanni.

"Hi, Yanni, and yes, I'm home and safe. I'm sorry I forgot to call, I was dead on my feet"—she immediately wished she hadn't used those particular words—"and I'm half-asleep."

"Any trouble on the way home?

"No. The drive was uneventful, just the way I like it. It was really pretty, though, with the moonlight on the snow. Actually, I enjoyed it."

"Do you need anything?"

"No, thanks, I'm good, and I'm ready for bed."

He took the hint and said good night. Before ringing off, he added, "Keep in touch, okay?"

"Will do."

Viridienne gently heaved DT off her lap and put her knitting back in the basket beside her chair. It really was time for bed.

Chapter Fifty-Six

The man, now back inside the car on the side of the road, sat thinking for a few minutes. Part of him wanted to get this whole thing over with. He was feeling the same desperate urgency he'd felt in the days before he killed Rose, but he also knew it wasn't time yet. If he moved in too fast, he could make a mistake, and a mistake could undo everything. Also, the planning and preparation—deadly foreplay—were the part of the game that he most enjoyed. When the final act was achieved, it was almost an anticlimax.

No. He would take the time necessary to do it right. That was how he did things. *Slow and steady wins the race.* Only it wasn't a race, and he was no longer steady. This would be—should be—the last run.

Chapter Fifty-Seven

T
hursday was usually the busiest day of the week at the Mayflower Gallery. Several classes were running at the same time, the artisan shop was open, and a weekly studio-painting group met from ten until three.

It all seemed so normal, and it *was* almost normal, or quickly getting there. People could feel awful for just so long, and then the wheels would start to turn, and the machine would get moving and begin to right itself. It was not that anyone felt any less devastated by the events of the previous week, but things needed doing, and everyone knew that work, even if it was mundane and repetitive— emptying the trash, even cleaning the bathrooms—could be healing.

When the delicate subject of a second cache of Rose's teaching supplies came up at a volunteer meeting, Jackson Smith volunteered to clean her classroom supply closet and sort what needed to stay as general supplies from what needed to be returned to the family. "I won't throw anything away. I'll just divide everything into piles and let someone else decide. I know that Viridienne already took her notebooks and her sketchbooks and stuff. This is just still-life supplies and reference books. But still...."

"Good idea," said Pauline. "You get it all together, and I'll ask Viridienne to look it over when you're finished. She'll know what to do."

BY MIDMORNING, VIRIDIENNE HAD FOLDED AWAY HER somber mourning clothes and was back in her loose-fitting dark pants and belted tunic. She was taking the faster, more direct highway route back down to Providence. In the cold grey rational light of dawn, over a second cup of coffee, she decided it might be wiser and more prudent to check out the Brandosis in the Providence Gallery before going down to New York. She would think of it as a practice run—she'd casually gather information without disclosing who she was or why she was doing it. If asked, she would be Valerie Stone, but she really hoped that wouldn't happen.

The gallery was not, as she might have expected, on the street with most of the galleries, artisan boutiques, and trendy restaurants but was on a side street. Viridienne was impressed by the quiet elegance of the long, clear windows and simple black-and-gold signage. The interior décor repeated the theme of *less is more*—neutral walls and carpeting and spare, functional furniture rather than the faux-French-provincial elegance and artfully worn Oriental carpets that so many upscale galleries considered essential to the trade.

Something inside her mind told her to park a couple of blocks away rather than right out in front. It could have been Yanni or Fitz—or perhaps Rose herself—warning her to be careful. Either way, Viridienne took the hint.

She was flushed and slightly out of breath from walking in the cold when she stepped through the door into Gallery 57. The place appeared to be empty. There was no one sitting behind the desk. Soft music was coming out of somewhere, and there was a faint smell of sandalwood in the air.

"Can I help you?"

Startled, Viridienne spun around to see a man standing behind her, shorter than she and with an olive skin tone not unlike Yanni's. Like most men who worked in upscale galleries, he was impeccably dressed. Over and above the sandalwood candle flickering on the desk, she could smell hair spray.

"Where did you come from?" she asked.

He chuckled. "I'm sorry. I didn't mean to scare you. The offices in this place are off to the side and not in the back like in most businesses. There's a door behind that half wall over there." He pointed. "I think I should put up a sign or something. It isn't the first time I've materialized out of the woodwork and come close to giving someone a heart attack." He gave another soft chuckle. "Back to my original question…" The man bowed and smiled. "How may I help you? Or do you just want to look around?"

"I think I just want to look around, thanks."

"Are you an artist?"

She wasn't prepared for such a direct approach.

"Why? Do I look like one?'

"Actually, you do. Remember, this is my business. I can spot an artist from a mile off. Are you looking for a gallery to represent you?"

She shook her head. "No, not really. Not now, anyway. I'm working on a research project. I decided to give myself the day off and go on a field trip."

"That's good, because we aren't taking on any other artists. I'm not sure how much you've looked into this particular gallery, but we only carry the works of the late Nicolo Brandosi. Our gallery and a larger one in New York are the only two galleries that carry his work. Do you know of him?"

By sheer force of will, Viridienne didn't so much as allow an eyelash to flicker in response to hearing the name. She just smiled. "Who in the art world hasn't? Actually, he's on the list of people I might consider for my project. That's why I came in today. But he's only one of many. I'm not sure if I want to restrict it to any one category other than postmillennial. I haven't even been accepted to a program yet, but I need to get some sort of an idea of what I want to do before I apply."

"Tell me, what is it about these people you haven't chosen yet that you'll be researching? What are the common threads?"

"TBA," she said, making air quotation marks with her fingers. "Something to do with what makes an artist transcend the trends and tastes of their own time and make it into the list of those whose work is considered more timeless and universal."

"That's a pretty tall order, but then, you are a pretty tall woman, if you'll pardon the little joke. I'm sure you are up to the task."

Viridienne was not amused. She'd been the target of teasing about her height for all of her life. "So I've been told." She gave him a plastic smile. "Actually, I'm still researching what I want to research, if that makes any sense, so I thought I'd start by seeing what's showing in big-name galleries right now."

"Living or dead?"

"I hadn't thought about that. First thought is both."

"You probably should decide before you actually begin. Meanwhile, go ahead and have yourself a good look around. Take all the time you need. If you do have a question, just come find me in the office. I'll be hiding in there, waiting to scare the bejesus out of another prospective customer."

This time, they both laughed. The soft-spoken, well-dressed gentleman retired to the office, and Viridienne did a slow walk around the gallery. Before leaving, she called out a thank-you and a cheery goodbye and carefully closed the door behind her against the cold.

―――――

At Plymouth Police Headquarters, Alison and Fitzpatrick were making more progress than they had dared hope for this early in the game. The pile of unpleasantness that Fitz had delivered to the forensic team had proved to be a veritable gold mine of DNA information.

That was the good news. The bad news was that it didn't
match anyone already on file.

"Still," said Fitz, who was always inclined to look on
the bright side of things, "when we do get lucky and get
ourselves a suspect, we'll test him on the spot."

"Not if he refuses, you won't," said the ever-practical
Alison.

"We have our little ways, my dear." Fitzpatrick was
leering and twirling an imaginary mustache.

Alison rolled her eyes. "I think it's time to see what we
can find out about the Brandosi family. Don't forget, we
really have a twofer going on here." She held up one finger.
"The murder of an artist who, by the way, was cranking
out paintings in her dead husband's name, which were
then being collected by someone in the know and undoubt-
edly connected to the family." She raised a second finger.
"And the whole art-fraud thing. They're connected, but
they are really two separate cases and investigations."

"So if we can find out who was coming around and
collecting the 'undiscovered Brandosis'—and of course, it
would be someone she knew—then we have a giant piece
of the puzzle."

She nodded. "The sticky part comes with finding that
piece and then finding where it fits."

"I think it's time to contact the Providence PD and put
our collective heads together."

She made a thumbs-up then wiggled it back and forth.
"That would be the most logical step, but from what I hear,
the mob in Providence has its tentacles woven into everything, and what's worse, they all seem to be fine with it. I
mean, if a convicted mayor can get reelected while he's

serving time in jail, how much luck do you think we're going to have asking questions that could upset a very complicated and nasty applecart?"

"You have made an excellent point, Dr. Watson. Nonetheless, it's a stone we must not leave unturned."

"Wait a minute, here—so you're Sherlock, and I'm the underling?" She drummed her fingers on the arm of the chair.

"Watson was hardly the underling. He was the one who did most of the mystery solving."

"Right, and Holmes got all the credit. That's not fair… and I didn't know you were a mystery fan."

"Mystery and more, my friend. Lots more. Like I told you, we Irish play it close to the chest. And just for the record, you know more about me than anyone except me own"—he bowed his head and made the sign of the cross —"saintly mother."

"Jesus, Fitz." She was laughing as she spoke.

He crossed himself again. "Him too."

She instantly grew serious again. "This is going to take some time, you know. I mean, something as complex as this, with so many layers of intrigue and deceit, doesn't just unravel with a few phone calls."

"No shit," said Fitz.

Chapter Fifty-Eight

By late February, even though it was still winter, the lengthening days, higher sun, and unmistakable damp-earth smell outside Viridienne's house signaled that spring was not far off. After a seemingly endless day at the gallery and then running errands, Viridienne dragged herself through the door of her cottage and, without even removing her cape, fell into her chair. She'd been teaching all day and doing her best to find the heart to start up her own artwork, but that part of getting back to normal still evaded her. It had been well over a month since Rose's death, and she felt she was treading water—holding her head up but not moving forward. Over the passing weeks, in her spare time, instead of Viridienne weaving a new tapestry on her loom, her alter ego, Valerie Stone, was weaving together the bits and pieces of information she'd been gathering about the history and whereabouts of the Brandosi paintings.

When the murderer was caught and convicted, she would take her collected information to Fitz and Alison and then to the media. Only then would justice be fully served and Xenia's name and claim to the works she'd done over all those years rightfully restored.

She glanced at the woodstove then at the fridge. Something was missing. DT. She looked around for the cat. Usually, he would be camped out in front of the stove, or if the house got too cool, he'd wedge himself into a corner of the sofa. She knew he hadn't gotten out because she was the only one who could let him out, and she never did.

Not good. A cat would hide when it was sick or scared. She called him by his nickname, then by his full name, with no response and was about to heave herself back up out of her chair and start looking under and behind things when the door to her studio opened, and a man holding a gun walked into the room.

"He ran and hid when I came in. I assure you he's fine. I like cats."

Viridienne froze. It was the man from Gallery 57 in Rhode Island.

"Don't bother asking. I picked the lock. Years of training." He walked across the room and sat on the sofa facing her. "And the answer to the second question is, I've been following you for some time now. And then you walked through the gallery door and right into my arms. Talk about good luck." He paused and touched his fingertips to his chest. "How very rude of me. Allow me to introduce myself. I never did give you my name. I'm Giovanni Brandosi. You can call me Gino. I'm Nicky Brandosi's brother and Xenia's brother-in-law. I'm the man who visited her twice a year and collected the latest *undiscovered* paintings."

Viridienne's heart was pounding, and she was struggling to breathe. She closed her eyes and inhaled slowly to the count of ten.

"Better," he sneered.

"Does it really make any difference to you?"

"Actually, it does. I'd hate to have you pass out on me and miss out on everything I have so carefully planned."

"You killed her."

He closed his eyes and bowed his head in mute acknowledgment. "It didn't have to be that way, you know. I was in love with her."

Viridienne's heart and mind were racing. She was trapped, and she knew it. She was in the middle of nowhere with a killer. No one would hear her scream, and even if she could make it to the front door, she couldn't outrun him. *Keep him talking, like in the TV detective dramas.*

"You loved her?"

He nodded. "I met her before Nicky did. I was an art history and arts management major at RISD. But before I could even buy her a cup of coffee, Nicky moved in, and that was it. He was the older brother, the sainted one. His shit was ice cream. He had first pick of everything. Especially women."

"Ro—Xenia didn't tell me anything about her past."

"Bullshit, she didn't. Why the hell have you been snooping around the galleries? Unfortunately for you, you knew exactly where to go… and so did I.

If you hadn't been so determined, I might have given

you a pass, let it go that Xenia had a friend. I might have believed you were harmless. But when I saw you at the funeral, and later, when you walked into the 57 in Providence, I knew exactly who you were and why you were there. You wrote your own death warrant, girlie. And I'm here to deliver it."

Keep him talking. Viridienne clamped her hand over her mouth and bolted out of her chair.

"Sit down.'

"I'm gonna throw up."

"Sure you are."

Without missing a beat, she vomited, splashing the contents of her stomach all over his expensive shoes.

"Oh, Jesus, go, and don't lock the door, or I'll kick it in."

Gagging loudly, Viridienne raced for the bathroom, and minutes later, white faced and sweating, she returned, clutching a wet facecloth. "I think I'll be okay now."

"You gonna clean that up? It stinks." He pointed to the mess on the floor.

"I'll throw a towel over it."

"It'll still smell."

"It's the best I can do," she said.

When she was back in her chair, she looked at the man seated on her sofa, and she spotted DT's one eye glaring at him from over the books in the shelf behind him.

Keep him talking.

"Did you kill Nicolo too?"

"It was a tragic accident."

"You killed him."

"He killed himself. As far as I was concerned, he killed

himself the first day he hit her. Fucker bragged about it. I wanted to kill him right there and then, but I would have been careless and gotten caught. So I waited. I knew how to do it."

"They tried to accuse her of doing it."

"We fixed that. Dropped a word or two in the right ears. In case you haven't heard, we've got connections." He gave a vicious, guttural laugh. "If she went to jail, we'd have no more 'Brandosi' paintings. Xenia was the cash cow. Keep her alive, hide her away, pay her off, protect her family, and stop them from going after us, but above all, keep those paintings coming. She was our retirement account." He laid the gun on the cushion beside him and rubbed his thumb against his fingers, signaling money.

Viridienne shook her head. She was breathing more easily now. "So why did you kill her?"

"Basically, we had enough Brandosis to keep us going. It was working perfectly. Between sales and resales, we had millions now and for the foreseeable future. But the stupid woman started painting again. To the untrained eye, they were different. But to an art expert, a signature is a signature. She painted her own death warrant... and she told you everything, didn't she?"

Viridienne was shaking uncontrollably. She folded her arms across her chest in an attempt to keep her body still. *Keep him talking.*

"Did she ever know how you felt about her?"

He shook his head. "I never got a chance to find out. After Nicky died, I approached her again. I was just the friendly brother-in-law, comforting the grieving widow. Offered to help her—you know, try to open that old door?"

His face twisted. "She pushed me away with both hands. Dammit." His voice was shaking. "She had her chance. After that, I watched and waited, and on a snowy night in January, I closed the book."

"End of story?"

"Don't be stupid. There are two more chapters that I can think of. You're one of them. Then one way or another, the Greeks will go after me. You know, an eye for an eye, a tooth for a tooth. Blood demands blood where I come from. It'll just be a question of how long I can keep running. They'll get me in the end… and I really don't give a shit. It will save me the trouble of offing myself."

Gone was the suave, polished man she'd met in the gallery. Sitting in front of her was a hunted, haunted, dangerous man seeking revenge. Despite her fear, Viridiennc could almost feel sorry for him. Almost. *Keep him talking.*

"Was it just you two brothers?"

His face twisted. "Three. The baby brother was Sal. Salvatore. He had it made for him. Got everything he wanted with sugar on top. Nicky was the first son, the golden-haired boy, the one who could do no wrong, the man who would carry on the family name. Well, that didn't work out, did it? I'm the little piece of shit caught in the middle. Sal's… in construction, as we like to say. He's running the family business in that sector. Me, I deal in art —stolen, forgeries…" He paused. "And recently discovered Brandosis. Then there's the restaurant branch of the family and the sanitary engineers, aka trash collectors. We've pretty much got it all covered."

A wood-splintering crash and a blast of cold air ended the conversation.

"Don't move or I'll shoot. I mean it. Leave the gun right where it is, and put your hands on top of your head." Fitz, having kicked in the door, was standing beside her, his gun pointing at Gino. And then he fired.

Chapter Fifty-Nine

Detectives Grey and Fitzpatrick and Viridienne Greene were sitting in the living room of Viridienne's cottage. A wounded, but by no means dead, Giovanni Brandosi was on his way, under guard, to the local hospital and, from there, to the Plymouth County Correctional Facility. The three of them were sitting at the table, eating Doritos out of the bag and drinking instant hot chocolate. Comfort food.

"Before I can declare this case closed, I just have to ask, how did you manage to puke on demand?"

She smiled. "A little trick I learned back in my youth at the compound. When they forced me to eat food I hated, I got it down, and as soon as I could leave the table, I got rid of it. A well-placed finger in the back of the throat… and upsy-daisy. Good to know I haven't lost my touch."

"Jaysus, woman. The man was going to kill you, and here you are an hour later, joking about it. It's not funny."

"Laughing to keep from crying, Fitz. I was scared out of my socks."

"Scared, but you didn't panic," said Alison. "You're something else."

"Believe you me, I wanted to. Maybe I was holding on for Rose, or maybe Rose was holding onto me. I guess I'll never know... and then you came busting through the door. The conquering hero." Her voice dropped to a more serious tone. "Thank you for saving my life, Fitz."

"Uh, sorry about the door."

The shattered door and frame had been covered over with a sheet of plywood and the cracks stuffed with yarn and fabric scraps. Not a thing of beauty, but it did the job.

"Doors can be replaced, Fitz. Meanwhile, we can come and go through the screened porch until I can get it fixed. I'm pretty good with a hammer."

"You're pretty good with a number of things, Ms. Greene. I admire you."

LATER, DRIVING BACK TO HEADQUARTERS, FITZ AND Alison were companionably winding down.

"Jesus, Fitz. Talk about arriving in the nick of time. What the hell made you go out there? Or maybe I shouldn't ask." She winked.

He shot her a dark look. "More like saved by the bell, partner. Would you believe she called me? I'd given her my private number to use in case of emergency. She faked the upset stomach and texted 'help' from the bathroom. She never took off her cape when she came in, and her phone was in her pocket."

"Damn quick thinking on her part."

"Good thing I picked up. I almost didn't. I thought it was my mother until I looked at the number. I got there in the nick of time, shot him in the leg, and saved the day. Call me Captain Marvel."

She laughed and then grew serious. "Now what? What'll happen to Brandosi the younger?"

"He's gone for good."

"Well, that was easy, wasn't it? She did most of the work for us. Maybe we should put her on the payroll."

"Considering that Providence PD turned tail and ran, you're probably right."

"What do you mean, turned tail?"

"I called the Providence chief the other day and asked for their cooperation on the investigation. But when I said it involved the Brandosi family, there was a long silence. Then he said it was our case, and they would help where they could, but since it was out of their jurisdiction… yada yada yada… yeah, right. The brotherhood of silence."

Fitz realized he'd been unconsciously clenching and unclenching his fist. "He almost fucking killed her, Alison." Fitzpatrick was not often given to swearing.

Chapter Sixty

Are you my sister? Looking for a tall woman in her late thirties or early forties who is interested in art. She left a religious group in Northern California ten years ago. If any part of this describes you or someone you know, please contact me at thinkless@jingo.net. My real sister left me a note the night she disappeared. My real sister will know where she left it and what it said.

Chapter Sixty-One

The man in the shadows was off the streets and would likely be locked away in the shadows of his own misery for the rest of his life. That part of the case—the stolen, forged, and black-marketed artwork and concomitant murders—was closed for good… or until such a time as a warring opposite family member, bent on revenge, set off to even the score.

As far as Detectives Fitzpatrick and Grey were concerned, there was one last *t* to be crossed: the three paintings that Alison and Fitz had taken from the gallery on the day after the murder. They were still in custody, so to speak, and needed to be released and returned to the family.

"Field trip to Providence?" said Alison brightly, leaning forward on her elbows and wiggling her fingers in the air. "It's a beautiful day. A touch of spring in the air. I volunteer myself. I remember how to get to the family's house. The fresh air would do me a world of good."

"Not so fast, there, partner. I think we should ask Viridienne first."

"Oh, you do, do you? And what might she have to do with it? They're not hers. They belong to Rose's family."

Fitz stammered. "I, uh… well… I thought maybe she'd like to see them one more time before we take them back… maybe even come with us when we take them back."

"Jesus, Fitz."

He blushed. "Don't forget Mary and Joseph."

"I'll call Viridienne, but let me handle it, okay?"

"But—"

"Boundaries!"

Fitz muttered something, and Alison did not ask for clarification.

Chapter Sixty-Two

❧

The days following what Viridienne was now referring to as "the home invasion" were filled with nightmarish flashbacks—so much so that she went online, googled PTSD symptoms, and checked every one. Every site suggested seeking medical or psychological help and not sitting silently with the pain. *Maybe later.*

The murderer was caught and charged and awaiting trial, and she had a new glass-and-steel front door. It was wonderful for light and triple glazed for heat retention. DT had come out of hiding and was handsomer than ever. Certainly heavier. The recent criminal activity inside his house had done nothing to curb his enthusiastic appetite.

In odd moments at the gallery, she and Jackson found themselves comforting each other by remembering Rose and sharing anecdotes. It was clear that he was missing her. Whenever possible, she took over and found odd jobs and errands for him to do, thereby filling some of the void in his life and giving him something else to think about.

But the artwork, her own lifeblood, hovered beyond her grasp. It would come one day, but until it did, she concentrated on her house—painting, cleaning, and scouring secondhand stores for scraps and treasures she might use in future creations. It helped to pass the time, but the flashbacks continued, becoming more and more vivid and intrusive and expanding to include memories of the Society of Obedient Believers. On a clear morning in late March, on one of her "awfuller" days—a word Rose like to use when things were going off the rails—Viridienne hit bottom. She was beginning to believe she was really losing it when three things happened in rapid succession that changed everything.

The first was a telephone call from Yanni, inviting her to come to the burial service in Providence in two days' time. The second was the decision to get professional help for the nightmares—and the daymares—that would not stop and were getting worse. The third, was a phone call from Alison Grey, telling her about the paintings that needed to be sent back to the Stamos family and asking if she would like to see them one more time before they were returned.

"Now, there's a coincidence," said Viridienne. "Just this morning, I got a call from Yanni, telling me the graveside service and burial will be held on the day after tomorrow and asking me to attend with the family."

"Are you going?"

"Of course… and I can take the paintings. They'll fit in the back of my car if I put the back seats down. Do you want me to come in and get them? Probably do me a world of good to get out."

"Have you not been going out?" asked Alison.

"Other than for my classes, no. I just haven't got the heart to do much of anything these days."

"Are you having trouble sleeping?"

"A better question would be, am I sleeping? And the answer is, not very much. Everything keeps replaying in my head... Rose on the floor, that man in my house, pointing a gun at me... other stuff too."

"What other stuff?"

"Backstory, Alison. My stuff. Not for public consumption."

Alison paused. "Viridienne, why don't you come in here and get the paintings? You say when. I'll make us some coffee or tea, and we can talk about what's happening and how you might be able to get some help with it. How about it?"

Viridienne sighed. "I guess it can't hurt. I thought about calling someone to talk to, but who would I call? It's not like I don't have any friends—well, actually, I don't. Rose was my one true friend. I do have people I have coffee with, and there are people at the gallery I have lunch with sometimes. I think about calling one of them, but I don't."

"When would you like to come in and get them? Is tomorrow morning good? How about ten thirty?"

"That works. I don't have any classes that day, and it will give me a little time to just sit with the paintings before I bring them back. They were the last ones she did, you know."

"I didn't know that," Alison said.

"And like I said, getting my butt out the door wouldn't be a bad thing, either. Thank you for suggesting this, Alison. I'll see you tomorrow morning."

WHEN ALISON DISCONNECTED THE CALL, FITZ WAS ALL eyes and ears. "What was that all about? Talk about *boundaries*. We don't do counseling here… although I'll be the first to admit that I think the woman needs help. PTSD?"

"Sounds like it. And no, we don't offer counseling, but we do make referrals. If anyone needs an intervention, it's her, and I think it has to be a woman."

Fitz chewed on his lip.

"I suspect you'll have an opportunity to plead your case in the future, boyo, but I suggest you wait until she is on steadier ground."

"Why do you always know so much about women, Alison?"

"Because I am one, and I'm not Irish."

"What the hell does that have to do with the price of fish?" Fitz asked.

"I speak up, and I speak out."

"So I've noticed."

IN PROVIDENCE, YANNI STAMOS HAD BEEN BUSY ALL morning, making the heart-wrenching final arrangements for his sister—quiet, private, for immediate family only. In addition to all of that, there was the convoluted matter of settling her estate. Surprisingly—or maybe not, considering how deliberately his sister lived her life—Xenia had dutifully registered a last will and testament three years before she died. But of course, when that document was signed and notarized, she was not the possessor of the entirety of her own work. What had been her property then—little more than a house, a plot of land, and some furnishings in downtown Plymouth—was now a multimillion-dollar enterprise with galleries, museums, and collectors already hammering at the door.

"It will all be settled in due time, and when it is, you will be the first to know," he repeated more times than he could count.

* * *

WITH SOME TIME TO HERSELF, VIRIDIENNE DECIDED TO take matters into her own hands. Perhaps it was the call from Alison, perhaps it was the fact that once Rose was returned to the earth, it really would be over, and she could begin to move on. Whatever the reason, she heaved herself out of her chair, wrapped her cape around her, and walked out the door and into the spring. The air was cool, not cold, and the sun was warm on her face. The ice was long gone from the pond, and at night, the chorus of screaming spring peepers—called "pinkletinks" by some—was unbelievably loud, considering how small those little frogs really were.

She remembered as a little child, before entering the society, putting on her boots and going out with her mother and father, looking for signs of spring—pussy willows, skunk cabbage, fiddleheads, and the rich earth-wormy smell of mud. Good memories, for a change. She reached up and snapped up a few pussy-willow wands. And on the way back into the house, she smiled into the sun and broke off a couple of branches of budding forsythia. Absolutely nothing said "spring" more definitively than a mason jar full of exploding forsythia on the kitchen table.

Chapter Sixty-Three

It was ten fifteen in the morning, and Fitz and Alison
were just finishing up after the daily briefing.

"So how do you want to handle this, Alison?"

"Play it by ear… but this here is what my ear is telling
me. I think we start all together. You, me, Viridienne, and
coffee. Keep it casual. I will ask about the burial, how she's
getting on, the cat, anything to get her talking and relaxing.
Then I ask you to go out and get the paintings. Take your
time. Then, when you bring them in, you need to find
something very important to attend to outside the office
and leave us alone for a while so we can talk. I'll shoot you
a text when it's time to come back in. That okay
with you?"

He saluted.

"Good, because I hear someone walking toward the
office. Remember, casual, easy, and for God's sake, stop
blushing."

Viridienne entered, greeted them both, swirled off her cape, and dropped into a wooden visitor's chair. "Did someone mention coffee yesterday?"

"I'll get it. Coffee making is man's work around here. Black, no sugar, right?"

They all laughed politely. After the coffee and the pleasantries, Fitz, on cue, went off and returned with the paintings, positioning them carefully along the long wall in the office. Viridienne swallowed a sob and looked away.

"Do you want to be alone with them for a while?" asked Alison. "I can step out for a little bit."

Viridienne nodded. Alison herded Fitzpatrick out ahead of her and quietly closed the door behind her, leaving the quiet, thoughtful woman with some time to herself and her memories. After a little while, she returned, tapped on the door, and quietly let herself back in to the room. Fitzpatrick was nowhere to be seen, and Viridienne was somber faced but in control. Alison stood in silence and looked at the paintings.

"You know, I never really looked at them as art. They were evidence, as far as I was concerned, and nothing more. I know zip about art. It's pretty or it isn't. That's it. But even I understand what everyone sees in her work. I can't put it into words, but it's as if they are reaching out to me, inviting me in to have a look around. Is that weird or what?"

"Not at all. Good art is a dialog. First, it's a dialog between the artist and the canvas—or in my case, the fabric and the fibers—and when the piece is finished, it's a dialog between the work and the viewer. As far as I'm concerned, if a piece of art doesn't make you curious, it has nothing to say. It's nothing more than something that fills an empty space. Rose's work speaks volumes. It always has."

"Wow." Alison drew up a chair and sat close to Viridienne. "Do you mind if I ask you about something you said yesterday? About the flashbacks? You said there was even more than the murder and the gunman. Would you like to tell me about it?"

Viridienne shrugged, blew her nose, and began to tell the story of her experience in the compound of the Society of Obedient Believers. She talked about deprivation, humiliation, and finally, what had happened on a night that no one talked about.

Detective Alison Grey, holding her hand in both of hers, listened to every word. "Dear God, woman. You have been violated in every sense of the word. Then as if that wasn't enough, you find the one woman you finally dared to trust dead on the floor, and the man who killed her breaks into your house, wanting to kill you too. That's enough to give anyone nightmares."

Viridienne nodded.

"I have worked with abuse victims for over fifteen years, and I know how and where to get you the help you need." She paused. "Would you like me to take you there?"

Viridienne gave another nod, then she whispered, "There's something else. I have a younger sister. I don't know whether she's still in there or whether she did what I did and got the hell out of there. I left her a note when I left. I told her if she ever wanted to find me, I would be on the East Coast. Not much to go on, is it? Maybe I should have kept my Obedient name, but I just couldn't."

Alison held up an index finger. "How computer savvy are you?"

"*Mezza mezza*. I do email, and I can Skype. And I know how to use a camera to help me with design and composition and to record images I might like to work on later."

"Are you on Facebook or Twitter or any other social media? Have you heard of Ancestry.com or looked on some of the genealogy sites?"

She shook her head. "No. I always thought it would be a waste of time."

Alison clapped her two hands together in affirmation. "This is for another day, but I think I can help you. At least get you started. It's not hard once you get the knack of it. And I'll show you the privacy and anonymity tricks too. But like I said, you've had enough for one day. Let's talk about this next time."

Viridienne nodded as Alison continued.

"Are you okay to go back home with the paintings, or would you like to have us deliver them to your place just before you leave for Providence tomorrow?"

"No, Alison, if you don't mind, I think I'd like to be alone and just sit with them for a day. I'll be okay. And by the way, I turned some kind of a corner yesterday... I went outside and picked some pussy willows and forsythia and smelled the mud. Things might finally be moving on."

As if on cue, Fitz tapped on the door and walked into the office.

"Oh good, just in time. I think we should help Viridienne load the paintings into her car so she can get back and get a good night's rest before tomorrow. It's going to be a long day for her."

Viridienne flashed a grateful smile. "Thanks to you, Alison, not as long as it might have been. I'll get in touch with you both the day after tomorrow."

Chapter Sixty-Four

T he burial was scheduled for eleven that morning. Viridienne gave herself plenty of time to get the paintings back into the car and make it down to the family home well before the appointed hour. The plan was to go from there to the funeral home, follow the hearse to the cemetery in their own cars, and after the ceremony, return to the house for coffee and sandwiches.

As she drove south in the bright morning sun, she was surprised to feel so much at peace with herself and the world around her. The paintings were stacked safely in the back, cushioned with blankets, and Viridienne was taking them home. She was closing a chapter of her life, saying goodbye. And for the first time since Rose had died, she was looking forward to the rest of the day and the days and weeks after that. The miles and the memories wrapped themselves around her, and despite her tragic reasons for making this journey, she found herself humming and smiling into the sunlight.

THE GLEAMING CASKET HAD BEEN POSITIONED OVER THE open grave and the mound of fresh earth next to it covered by a shroud of green AstroTurf. At a signal, about twenty people dressed in black, most holding a single white rose, gathered around the casket. The priest stood at the head, and on either side of him stood the family—the two older brothers, their wives and children, Xenia's father on the arm of Yanni, and Viridienne holding onto Yanni's other arm. The funeral directors stood side by side, in attendance but discreetly out of the way.

The ritual was brief, and the casket was lowered, then family members, one by one, stepped up to the grave to toss a handful of earth and a white rose down onto the shadowed casket. Viridienne weeping openly, took her turn amongst the others with Yanni close beside her.

And then it was over. After a few moments of whispered words of prayer and consolation, they slowly trickled back to their cars. The midday sun, brilliant and beautiful and full of the promise of spring, was high and warm on their backs. A light lunch, already set out, awaited them at home, and they were more than ready for it.

By early afternoon, everyone but the brothers and their wives had left the house, and Viridienne was preparing to do the same when Yanni held up his hand and asked her to stay on for a little while longer.

"There's something that needs clearing up," he said.

"I don't understand. I thought this was the final chapter." She didn't want to bring up any of the sordid details of Xenia's death.

"Come in and sit down with us." He guided her back into the living room and over to the chair he knew she liked.

Dimitri, Xenia's oldest brother opened the conversation. "I don't suppose you knew it, but a couple of years ago, Xenia, in her very organized way, made a will wherein she stated her wishes as to the deposition and distribution of her money and material goods. This was worded to include all of her paintings, which are now rightfully attributed to her and worth millions. She stated that the paintings—her own and those painted in the Brandosi name—if ever recovered, were to become the property of her family of origin. Her money, not much, was to be equally divided amongst the nieces and the nephews."

Viridienne was taking all of this in and wondering why she had been included. Yanni had said she was family, but still, the conversation was feeling way too intimate for her comfort. She shifted and glanced over to Yanni, who smiled.

"The final consideration of her real and personal possessions"—Dimitri was looking directly at Viridienne —"is her house in Plymouth, which she has willed in its entirety, along with funds for taxes and upkeep for as long as she wants to live in it, to her best friend and confidante, Viridienne Greene."

Viridienne sat wide-eyed and dumbstruck while the rest of the people in the room erupted into smiles, tears, cheers, and applause.

He continued. "Viridienne, you gave our sister something we couldn't give her—someone to talk to, someone to be there. And you almost got yourself killed in trying to restore her rightful name to the paintings. So to you, Viridienne Greene, Greek in everything but appearance"—a warm chuckle rippled gently through the room—"we are grateful and honored to give you these." He crossed the room and stood in front of Viridienne. "Hold out your hand."

She did as instructed, and Dimitri, with a grand flourish, placed a set of house keys into her open hand. "We've had it completely restored and painted, and it's ready for you to move in whenever you want."

"And another thing…" said Yanni. "We want you to take back one of those three paintings that you brought with you today. You can choose which one. If anyone in the world deserves to have one of her paintings, it's you. Xenia is dead, and we can't bring her back, but in the space she left, she gave us you."

"I… oh gosh, uh…"

"Would you like a glass of water?" he asked when the formalities were finished.

"I think I would like a glass of wine. A glass of retsina. A big one."

Chapter Sixty-Five

It was dark when Viridienne returned to her cottage by the pond and walked in through her newly installed front door. DT was giving her *the look*, and she knew her first responsibility was to fill his food dish and give him fresh water. "Here you go, big boy. Have at it." She straightened up and sniffed the air. The cat box could wait.

She made herself a cup of chamomile tea, and while it was steeping, she rummaged around in the fridge for something she could eat cold, right off the shelf. With that accomplished, rather than flopping into her favorite spot, she set her food, a pad of paper, and a pencil on the table then pulled up a chair, leaned forward, and rested her aching head in her hands.

Her brain felt like a pinball machine on steroids. From the moment she left the Stamoses' house, questions, possibilities, and challenges bombarded her from all directions. *Sell the big house and keep the little one? Live in the big one and rent the little one? Sell the little one. NO!* And rumbling around underneath all of them was the biggest question of all: Did she really want to live in the house where her best friend was killed—or even want to set foot in it again? The memories, the recent ones anyway, were bad recurrent dreams.

And then, of course, underneath all of that, was the faded image of her little sister, who would be a grown woman by now. *Where are you?*

She was starting to reach for her teacup when her phone rang.

"Viridienne? It's Alison Grey. I've found your and your sister's birth records in Crescent City, California. No death record, so we know she's alive. It's not much, but it's a beginning. Can you come into the station tomorrow afternoon? I'm going to give you a crash course in Internet research and social media and see what we can do about finding her and contacting her."

When Viridienne didn't answer, Alison asked, "Viridienne, are you there? Are you okay?"

"I'm here… and I'm okay. Just overwhelmed. It's just been a very long day, and I don't have too many words left in me. All I can say right now is thank you… thank you. I'll fill you guys in on everything when I come in tomorrow. What time shall I come over?"

REPOSTED: ARE YOU MY SISTER? LOOKING FOR A TALL woman in her late thirties or early forties, interested in art, who left a religious group in Northern California some time ago. If any part of this describes you or someone you know, please contact thinkless@jingo.com. My real sister left me a note the night she disappeared. My real sister will know where she left it and what it said.

REPLY: THIS IS A LONG SHOT, BUT I MET AN ARTIST some time ago who said she had been a member of a religious cult in California when she was young. I'll see if I can remember who it was or if I still have her card. If I do, I'll be in touch.

WHEN SHE COULD BREATHE NORMALLY AGAIN, EMILY picked up her laptop and raced into the kitchen to tell Donna and show her the message.

"Well, lordy, lordy, lordy," said Donna, wrapping her in a giant hug. "It's not much, but it's a whole lot more than we had an hour ago, which was a whole lot of nothing." She closed one eye and held up her finger. "I do believe this calls for a piece of pie. I hid one away from the kids after supper last night. I'll go cut it in half. You pour the milk."

Chapter Sixty-Six

Viridienne climbed into bed, pulled up the blankets, stretched out, and stared at the ceiling. DT, the self-appointed fuzzy sleeping pill, crash-landed beside her and kneaded himself a comfortable spot within easy patting distance before launching into a rumbling, comforting purr. He had a job to do.

Well after eight the next morning, she unglued her eyes, and the cat was still there. She reached down and scratched his massive head then trailed her fingers down under his chin for a good tickle. Only when she stopped did he jump down and set up a piteous wail beside his empty food dish.

"Okay, kiddo," she said, rubbing the sleep out of her eyes and swinging her feet to the floor. "You've earned yourself a double with a side of treats." Only when she'd made the little joke to her cat, did she realize she was finally on the mend. "Too much to think about, cat boy, but fresh coffee will help me get started." It was indeed a new day.

———

LATER THAT AFTERNOON, WITH HER LAPTOP IN HAND AND looking hopeful, Viridienne sat down at a coffee-scarred oak table with Detectives Fitzpatrick and Grey. "Before we get started on the technical stuff, I need to ask a question."

"Go for it," said Alison.

"Well, I don't know quite how to say it, but it seems to me that you two have gone over and beyond what I would have expected of two detectives investigating a murder. I feel like I'm getting special treatment... and I don't really need to know why I'm getting all this personal attention, but I do want to say thank you. And if there isn't a reason, and this is how you treat everyone who is a witness to a murder, well, then, thank you anyway."

Fitz started to speak, but Alison interrupted him. "Let me answer that, Fitz. Yes, we are doing more than we ordinarily would do. Police often go beyond the line of duty... but we don't say a lot about it when we do. It's something to do with professional boundaries. Fitz knows what I'm talking about."

Fitz rolled his eyes, and Viridienne looked even more perplexed.

"It goes without saying that you had an awful experience, and we both knew it and wanted to help, so we did our job the best we could. And you helped us do that job by being honest and telling us anything you could. Then when you told us the rest of the story about your own background and wanting to find your sister, I knew there was something more we could do."

"But we couldn't do it on company time," said Fitz. "So Alison gets the brilliant idea of helping you with the search for your sister after hours. We have access to information that the man on the street will never even know about."

"And I got started yesterday afternoon. It didn't take long to find the birth records for Annamarie Jorgenson— your original name—and the registered change to Obedient Charity. Right on the same page was Obedient Thankful, your sister. I have to tell you that is one mother lode of a name to be stuck with."

"I became Viridienne Greene two months after I turned eighteen."

Alison powered up her computer and turned toward Viridienne. "Well, then, let's get started."

Fitz made a hasty sign of the cross before opening his own device. He and Alison were unsure of what they would find and equally unsure of what would happen if they did find something.

Chapter Sixty-Seven

Viridienne took a deep breath and squeezed both hands into tight fists for courage. *Hanging onto heaven knows what—just hanging on.* It was the first time she'd been anywhere near the place since the day she witnessed firsthand the vicious destruction that a single obsessed, vengeful man wreaked upon its stately Victorian elegance. Now she was the owner.

She stood on the front porch, set the cat carrier down at her feet, and pulled the key that Yanni's brother had given her out of her pocket. The spring-warm, late-afternoon sun cast a patchwork of moving shadows from the overhanging trees on the boards beneath her feet. She was trying to decide whether this was a final chapter or the prologue to a new book. *Should I laugh or cry?* The gods and goddesses, in their quixotic fashion, had presented her with a not untypical dilemma.

Her best friend was gone. Her murderer had been identified, found guilty, and incarcerated. Justice, in its poetic and sometimes incomprehensible way, had been served. Rose's true name, Xenia Stamos, was restored to the paintings and to her estate, and all future sales and royalties were rightfully in the hands of her family… and their lawyers. Rose-Xenia was dead, but she had a continuing legacy. Her name and her paintings would go on living.

And then there was the house. This house… now her house. The last time she'd seen it, it had been a complete wreck. The floors were soaked, the furniture, mirrors, pipes, and plumbing fixtures smashed, and art supplies stomped on and ground into the rubble. And there was a smell she cared not to remember.

When the Stamos family got word of what had happened to it, they moved fast. They hired a disaster-restoration company to clear out the mess and take the place down to the studs… and then restore it. "The bones of the house are still solid," they told Yanni, who'd put himself in charge of the project. "Such a beautiful old place should not be destroyed. And once restored, it will be worth a fortune."

Now it was hers—a house with eleven rooms, five working fireplaces, a finished attic, a stone foundation, front and back porches, a furnace that needed replacing, and a kitchen that still had the original soapstone sink. A house with all of its present and future expenses, including taxes and regular maintenance, covered by the trustees of the estate of the late and much beloved Rose Doré. A house that, after its vicious destruction, had been freed of the anger and filth that almost brought it to its knees. Its dignity and elegance were restored, and it stood empty, waiting for its new owner.

The memories, good and horrific, tumbled over each other in her mind. She knew damn well she could walk through that familiar front door, but she was not prepared for just how hard the first time was going to be.

"Hey there. Fancy meeting you here. I… uh… was just passing by, and I saw you standing there. Do you need a hand?"

Startled, she whirled around to see Fitz. She was pleased and irritated. *It's called ambivalence. It's a familiar feeling these days.* "What are you doing here? I didn't hear you pull up. You startled me. I'm still pretty jumpy, you know."

"Sorry. Plymouth is a small town—you know that. Word gets around. A transfer of property is a matter of public record. I work for the town. Thought I'd drive by and just make sure no one had revandalized the place or anything… and JMJ, look who's here—your very own self. Would you like me to come in with you?"

By way of response, she smiled and held up her hand. "With all due respect, Fitz, that's very kind of you, but why ever would you want to?"

He cocked his head. "Intuition, maybe? I don't know. Your best friend died in there. You found her. Might be a little hard to walk through the door the first time. Not to mention, with all these months that it's been being shoveled out and restored… well, I just thought…" He smiled a little sheepishly. "I guess I just wanted to make sure you were all right."

Viridienne bit her lip to keep from bursting into tears

right in front of him. The gesture was so touching. So like him.

She smiled and reached for his hand and held it in both of hers. "Not this time, my friend. For reasons I can't even explain to myself, I need to walk through that door for the first time by myself, on my own two feet. Just me and the cat. Or maybe even just me… and then I'll come back for the cat."

He stepped back and looked up at her fondly. "Of course… I get it. It was thoughtless of me to even think of it."

"Fitz?" She looked down at him. "Do you really understand?"

"More than you know. But one day, maybe, I'll let you in on the secret."

"And what do you mean by that?"

"Classified information, madam. But let me come back sometime when you're settled in and I'm off duty, and we can discuss it."

"Good grief. Are you asking me out on a date?"

He shook his head, his freckled cheeks going crimson. "I'm not even sure if I know myself. Let's table the thought for the time being. The case is closed. Otherwise, this would be a complete breach of professional ethics… or maybe one mother of a long shot. We can discuss that too. Meanwhile, duty calls, but you be sure to call me if, when you get inside there all by yourself… that is, if you need anything."

"Thanks, Fitz, I will. I promise. Really."

"God bless you, woman, and good luck." He smiled,

turned on his heel, walked back to his car, waved, and drove off.

Viridienne watched him leave then turned the key in the old lock and pushed open the door. The house was empty and spotless. Her footsteps sounded twice as loud as they really were. All traces of the devastation, of Rose, of her furniture, her paintings, even her signature smells—linseed oil and Earl Grey tea—were gone. The place smelled like a new house—a freshly painted, very clean, elegant house. Her house…no… her home.

She turned, went back outside, and picked up the cat carrier. "Come on, animal. Let's see what you think of the place."

Chapter Sixty-Eight

A week later, Fitz pulled the black-and-white sedan to a stop outside the big old house and listened to the engine slowly tick itself down into silence. This was simply a courtesy call, he told himself, a wellness check, a marking off of the last box after formally closing the case. As a rule, police officers didn't make courtesy calls or wellness checks on a witness, but when he called and asked if he might drop by to see how she was getting on, she sounded genuinely pleased to hear his voice.

He rubbed his chin with one hand and drummed on the steering wheel with the fingers of the other. He was thinking about the sequence of events that had led to Viridienne's inheriting the house. It was odd, really. People in their forties and early fifties—in this case, the deceased, Rose Doré—didn't usually make out their wills at such an early age. On the other hand, nothing about this particular case had made any sense until the very end. And even then, Fitz still had questions.

The engine was quiet now, and he could hear the wind moving through the trees outside and above the car. He shook his head and called a halt to his internal meanderings. He was stalling. The ostensible reason for his coming to Viridienne's house was to check and see how she was doing... first week in the new house and all that. He'd called first just to make sure it was okay. *So why am I sitting outside, thinking about it instead of going up to the door and finding out?* Denial was a wonderful tool of both survival and protection, and Detective Inspector Patrick Shamus Fitzpatrick was making full use of it. He was feeling more like a fifteen-year-old on a first date than a thirty-four-year-old ten-year-veteran detective on the Town of Plymouth force. He was filled with teenaged anxiety, fear, and self-doubt while at the same time holding tightly to a sliver of what, in any other circumstance, might have been called hope. *After all, didn't she say yes to my request to drop in for a visit?*

Fitz was a romantic, a dreamer, and a closet poet, none of which were skills required for police duty. He knew nothing about the woman really. She was a lanky grey-haired fabric and fiber artist several years his senior, and he wanted so very much to see more of her. Fitz remembered his grandmother sitting in her chair, knitting sweaters and socks and eventually, as she aged, only endless scarves. He'd written a poem when she died. He'd won a prize with it. He thought back to when he first entered Viridienne's cottage on that snowy morning in January. He had done so with the intention of interviewing her as a witness to a murder and nothing more. He found the tangle of her yarns and threads piled here and there around the house curiously comforting. It made him think of his grandmother... he could almost smell her. Wood smoke, lavender, and strong tea. He was surprised to learn Viridienne lived alone with a one-eyed ginger tomcat who never left her side. And while she was friendly enough and spoke easily about her art, the house, and her cat—and eventually, even her murdered friend—she saved her personal history for later. On the_day she told them about the Obedient Believers and about her lost sister, he'd wanted to take her under his wing and protect her... or maybe more. That was an awkward thought. The woman was a full head taller than he was.

In their various conversations, she'd given the impression of being completely uninterested in adding anything or any*one*, in the shape of a significant other, to her life. *So what am I doing here?* He looked again at the house, made a hasty sign of the cross, and pushed open the car door.

The veteran detective said, "You're away with the fairies, man. This is not according to protocol." But the off-duty dreamer, romantic, and closeted poet, who was on his day off, won the argument. He tucked the supermarket bouquet of tulips under his arm and started toward the door.

***

You can look, but don't touch
A heart, your heart, breaks easily
And is not easily mended or fixed

By the likes of you.

You with your sticky-out ears and your clumsy hands and
your still scraped knees.

You're way too young and too dumb to be falling in love
Or are you?

Chapter Sixty-Nine

Viridienne was asking herself for the twentieth time, *Why the hell did I say yes?...* when the doorbell rang. She peeked out the window and saw Fitz shifting from one foot to another, looking like an awkward fifteen-year-old at his first school dance. Even through the window, she could see he was blushing and choking the life out of a bunch of tulips stuffed under his arm.

She took a deep breath, swallowed hard, and opened the door. "Right on time."

He went an even darker shade of red. "Can't help it. Twelve years of Catholic schools and four years of St. Michael's College. It's baked in." He held out the flowers. "Tulips are my mother's favorite. Figured I couldn't go wrong with them."

"Mine too," she said, accepting them and stepping back into the house. "Come on in, and I'll make you some tea—really strong the way you said you like it—and some coffee for myself... and get these right into a vase." She was talking way too fast, and she knew it.

"Don't forget to cut the stems before you put th—" He stopped just inside the door and looked left and right. "Wow! This place looks great. You've been busy."

"Not by half. Work is therapeutic. Hard work is very therapeutic. I still don't know what I'm going to do with all this space, but I suspect that will become manifest. Right now, it's me, a few sticks of furniture I had in the cottage, my cat, and a lot of empty rooms." She laid the tulips on the counter beside the sink.

Fitz smiled and dropped his jacket on the back of the nearest chair, no longer blushing. Her heartbeat had returned to near normal, and the cat, oblivious to all but the raw emotion, hopped up onto his own cushioned chair by the back door and watched as the two cautiously sat down at the kitchen table.

Viridienne got right to the point. "So, Fitz, why are you really here? Somehow, I don't think this is a court-ordered wellness check."

He nodded. "Right in one, madam. If the murder case were not closed, I wouldn't be here. But it is, and..." He looked down at the table.

She spoke softly. "And what, Fitz?"

He threw up his hands. "Oh, what the hell. I'm here because I would like to see you in a nonprofessional situation—like, maybe dinner and a movie or a Sunday drive someday."

"As long as you don't say walks on the beach and quiet evenings by the fire."

"And why would you say that?"

She laughed. "Okay, full disclosure. Once upon a time, I went on an online-dating site. Once and once only! And let me tell you, just about every man I looked at was looking for someone who loved animals and children and enjoyed quiet evenings by the fire and long walks on the beach. Oh, yes, and they put up pictures that were clearly half the age and the weight they said they were. I gave up before I even got started. Changing the subject, what did you major in at St. Michael's?"

He looked down and mumbled, "English and Irish poets of the nineteenth and twentieth century."

"You're kidding."

"I'm not. It's possibly the second most useless degree a man could have."

"What's the first?"

"Philosophy and religion."

She laughed, this time without restraint. "Okay, the obvious question: With that background, why did you go into law enforcement?"

"You want the truth?" he asked.

"Nothing less."

"Much as I love literature and poetry, I wanted to do something practical with my life besides pay the bills and eat. I didn't have the time, money, or inclination to study law. Too dry and technical for the likes of me. Law enforcement has any number of career options. There's a family history too. More than a few Boston Irish cops in my family."

"And…?"

His voice dropped to an almost whisper. "And when no one's looking, I write poems."

She hesitated. "Will you let me see them someday?"

"Possibly." He winked. "But back to the original question. What am I doing here? Well, I'm not half your age, but I am several years younger than you."

Viridienne responded without missing a beat. "And I'm half a head taller than you. Most men don't like to be seen with women older and taller than them."

"I guess they don't know you very well. Would you be willing to be seen with the likes of me, Viridienne Greene? Red-haired, freckle-faced Irishman, shorter than you and several years your junior?"

Viridienne tipped her head to one side and smiled at the hopeful-looking man sitting across the table from her. "I guess there's only one way to find out, isn't there? You're here, aren't you?"

"And now that we've got that out of the way, would you like that cup of tea I mentioned a while back? And after that, would you like a tour of the house? I mean, there isn't much to see but a lot of empty rooms right now. I have to set up a working studio, and I do have a real bedroom. My sofa bed from the cottage and a floor lamp is the sum total of my living room furniture. But it's a start. I'm a thrift-shop and yard-sale junkie, so I figure I can take my time and find exactly the things I want at a price I can afford."

"I'd like that very much. Two for tea and a tour for two. See, I told you I'm a words man. Oh, and while I think of it, Alison wanted me to ask if you had made any more progress on the search for your sister."

"Alison knows you're here?"

He gave her a sheepish grin. "You may remember me telling you that she knew more about me than my own

mother. Well, she does. She's the one who played chaperone and ran interference and kept me honest until we
closed the book on Brandosi."

"What do you mean?"

"She saw the sparks in the air and the handwriting on
the wall a long time before I did. Warned me off in no
uncertain terms, she did. Kept whispering 'boundaries' in
my ear."

"She did?" Viridienne asked. "And you listened?"

"I did."

"And now?"

"I'm here, and I've finished my tea. Did you say something about a tour of the house? It was not at its best when
last I saw it."

Viridienne got up from the table and pushed in the
chairs while Fitz collected their cups, rinsed them, and set
them in the drainer beside the sink. DT, still on his cushion, was more than curious about this stranger in the house
and followed his every move with his one big green eye.
Fitz reached down and gave him a friendly ear scratch on
his way by.

"So, you never said—have you made any progress in
finding your sister?"

Viridienne leaned back against the sink and folded
her arms across her chest. "Thank you for asking.
Thanks to Alison coaching me in the ways of Internet
searching, I might be getting closer. It's still very much in
the 'someone who knows someone who met someone
who thinks they might have heard something about
someone' stage, but I *am* getting responses, and I'm
following up on every single one. Alison is doing what

she can with her own resources after hours on the office computer."

He looked alarmed. "Jaysus, Viridienne, for God's sake, be careful. Internet predators just love finding someone like you."

She shook her head and waved him down. "Way ahead of you. As I said, I've been coached by the finest, your partner. I'm using a false name, and I've opened a temporary Yahoo account for that purpose only." She smiled. "Whatever happens, if I find her or I don't, I owe the two of you a dinner in a five-star restaurant for all the help you've given me. Meanwhile, come see the house."

After the tour, the two sat at opposite ends of the sofa with DT, the self-appointed chaperone, positioned exactly in the middle.

"Lots of potential, here, Viridienne. And while I might not be very bright or artistic, I can move furniture and do odd jobs when the need arises."

"I'm still working all of this out in my head. There's a lot to think about. I guess I didn't tell you, but along with the house, Rose set up a living trust that will cover the taxes and upkeep of this house for the rest of my life. Should I decide to sell it, the money from the house comes to me, and after paying any income taxes, the money in the trust reverts to her family of origin."

"JMJ, that's one hell of a gift."

"Tell me. It's a gross understatement to say I wasn't expecting it. Floored, speechless, and gobsmacked all at once."

Fitz chuckled. "That's quite an image, you know. But

really, do you have any long-term plans yet? This is a lot of house for one person both to live in and to manage."

Viridienne chewed on her lip before answering. "I figure I need a bedroom, a studio, a sitting room, and maybe some exhibit space, like Rose had, here on the first floor. That and a kitchen to cook and eat in. That leaves me three more bathrooms and five more spare rooms with nothing to keep them busy." She paused and gave him a half smile, "I'll tell you another secret. I've always had a secret dream of having an artist and writer's B and B."

"Another secret? What was the first one?"

"I already told you. My little sister. If I ever find her, one of those five rooms could be for her, and I'd still have four more."

Chapter Seventy

Reply: I think I might have found the person you are looking for. I don't have street address, but I met a woman that sounds like who you are looking for. Her name is Viridienne Greene or something like that. It's a color. I remember that she teaches weaving at the Mayflower Gallery in Plymouth, Massachusetts. If you call them, they might be able to help you. Good luck.

Chapter Seventy-One

I t was now full-blown forsythia-laden, daffodil-strewn, sweet-smelling New England spring. The world was alive again. Inside the lovely old house on Atherton Street, Viridienne was still getting used to her new surroundings, but she was fast gaining on it. She'd added more furniture and had looked up the rules and requirements for opening a B and B. She'd set up a working studio and was once again actively making her fiber-and-fabric creations and teaching her regular classes at the Mayflower Gallery. All that and more. Since that first awkward visit over tea at the kitchen table, she'd spent several happy hours in the company of a certain member of the Plymouth law enforcement team... and she'd connected with her sister.

Two weeks earlier, the convoluted "someone who knew someone who" email turned out to be the real thing. Less than a week later, they'd spoken—first on the phone, then on Skype—and now she was waiting at Logan Airport for the plane that carried her sister to land. Her mind was whirling with questions about all they had missed out on in the years since she escaped. *Where to begin? What to say? Will she like her room? What kind of food does she like… and what about Fitz? Where will he fit into this?*

When she'd voiced all these worries to Fitz, he said, "Just think of it as one of your creations, woman. You start where you think you should and then just keep working at it and see what happens. There aren't any rules for things like this. If anyone can weave it all back together, it's you."

She held onto those words as the digital sign announced that the plane had landed and through the agonizing wait until the passengers began to stream through the gate.

"Emily?"

"Viridienne?"

The two women flew into each other's outstretched arms and held on for dear life. After the hugs and the tears, Viridienne grabbed hold of some of her sister's luggage. "It's not far to the car. The drive to Plymouth is about an hour and twenty minutes. Your room is ready, and the Crock-Pot is full and holding on low, and the cat is probably standing guard at the door. We have all night and forevermore to catch up. Food first."

"Viridienne?"

"Mmm?"

"I still can't believe it." Her eyes were glistening.

"Believe it, sister. We did it… with a little help from our friends."

THANK YOU FOR READING. PLEASE SIGN UP FOR MY newsletter for notifications of new releases.

COMING SOON, THE **SECOND IN THE VIRIDIENNE Greene mysteries,**

The Deception Room. To learn more, check in on my Author page, **Judith Campbell Author**, or website, www.judithcampbell-holymysteries.com

.

———

JUDITH CAMPBELL ALSO WRITES, **THE OLYMPIA BROWN Mysteries,**

available on Kindle, in print, and on Audible.

THE FIRST IN THE SERIES IS, **A TWISTED MISSION**

Read on for a sneak peek

Sneak Peek, A Twisted Mission

Without warning the snake slashed and zigzagged across the path just inches from his feet. He almost stepped on it. With his heart racing and sweat breaking out everywhere, he watched as the moving grasses off to his right indicated the direction of the reptile's speedy escape.

He straightened up and looked around to see if anyone had witnessed the incident but saw no one. He was morbidly afraid of snakes and had been since the day his father, drunk and trying to make a man of him, threw one in his face and then laughed when he screamed, fell on the ground and wet himself. The only thing he feared more than snakes these days was someone finding out about it. This was a close call, but so far his luck was holding. No one saw it. His shameful secret was still safe. When his breathing and heart rate returned to normal, he continued walking along the sandy path toward the crew shack. To be on the safe side, he stamped his feet, flapped his arms and made as much noise and commotion as he could.

Across the street and up the short hill from the camp ground, a painfully thin and desperately unhappy young man scribbled a few words on a scrap of paper, folded it in half and pushed it deep into his jeans pocket. Then he climbed up on top of the battered old wooden dresser next to his bed. Careful to keep his balance, he tossed one end of a twisted sheet up and over the ceiling beam directly above him. He knotted it, yanked on it to test its strength and then secured it. Once that was done, he tied the other end around his neck. He had taken great care with the measurements so that when jumped off and kicked the shoddy dresser away from beneath him, his feet would not reach the floor. He hoped, even dared to pray, it would be quick.

A fiftieth birthday, whatever else it might be, is a milestone. It can be a warning signal, a turning point or both. It can be loudly celebrated or quietly ignored, but it cannot be denied. It is a time when many will choose to step back and take stock. The Rev. Dr. Olympia Brown had just reached that significant event with as many questions in her mind as she had years logged onto the calendar. The two at the very top of the list were, should she continue as a college chaplain and professor of humanities and religion at Merriwether College, or should she change direction, leave academia and take on a full time parish ministry?

On the nonprofessional and more personal front there

were more questions. Now that her two sons, Malcolm and Randall, were technically out of the safe suburban nest, her status as a not-very-swinging single was lonely. Maybe she should be more proactive about creating a little more action in that corner of her life. Maybe she should move out of her white, middle class, three-bedroom expanded cape in the town with the good schools that she needed when the boys were young and buy a condo in Boston or Cambridge. That would certainly ease her commute and save money on gas.

She could take her mother's advice, let nature take its course and wait for the universe to reveal what the future might offer—but Olympia rarely took her mother's advice, so she eliminated that one even before she wrote it down. And so it was on a spectacular summer day in early June, she was sitting in her back yard, sipping iced tea and making a list ... or maybe it was a five-year plan—she hadn't decided which. In big block letters she created three columns across the top of the sheet of paper: Done, Yet to be done, and Wishful thinking bucket list.

If nothing else, and there was a whole lot of else, Olympia Brown was methodical and well organized. She typically set reasonable goals for herself and then in her own determined fashion strategized how to reach them. At age fifty, she knew who she was and pretty much what she wanted out of life. She also knew what she was and was not prepared give up in order to bring that about, or so she thought.

However, nothing that was about to happen in the coming summer was on this list and no one, not even Olympia, the practical plotter, could have predicted or planned for what did happen. She couldn't possibly know it, but it seemed she was at the mercy of a host of gods and goddesses who were bored and decided to have a bit of fun. The object of their ungodly mischief of fancy and foolishness was a middle-aged, slightly restless college professor who in one unguarded moment said she might be ready for a change. She looked again at the sheet of paper in her lap, made a face, and scrawled, "None of the above." Then she crumpled the paper and tossed back and high over her shoulder.

She decided to take a second look at the invitation she'd received to be a summer chaplain at Orchards Cove in Maine. A summer of fresh sea air and camping under towering pines in a seaside village would be a refreshing change and give her plenty of time to think about her future. Would it not?

Olympia's mother also told her, "Be careful what you wish for." It would have been good advice, had she listened, but she didn't, and therein hangs the tale.

To read this book and to find other Olympia Brown Mysteries,   visit www.Amazon.com/OlympiaBrownMysteries.com   or www.UUA/Bookstore.org

They are also available in libraries, and if all else fails, contact the author at:

www.juithcampbell-holymysteries.com

About the Author

Rev. Dr. Judith Campbell is a community-based Unitarian Universalist minister. In addition to *Forgery in Red*, the first in the Viridienne Greene Mysteries, she has authored eleven—soon to be twelve—books in the Olympia Brown Mystery series. She has also published poetry, children's books, two books on watercolor painting, and several articles on religion, spirituality, and the arts. She lives by the sea in Plymouth, Massachusetts, with her husband, Chris Stokes, along with their two cats.

Writing is her passion, her challenge, and the most authentic way she can live into her ministry. What she attempts to do with her writing is to raise awareness around current social and ethical issues that affect us all... and therein hangs a tale... a very good tale.

Judith is available in person or on Skype to speak to your book group or at your library. As a minister and teacher, she is available to lead workshops and retreats on fiction, memoir, and spiritual biography. Please contact her and get on her mailing list through her website, www.judithcampbell-holymysteries.com, or through her two Facebook pages: Judith Campbell, and Judith Campbell Author. She loves to hear from her readers and responds personally to every email.

Made in the USA
Middletown, DE
09 June 2021